Ear Candy

A Charitable Endeavors Novel

M.E. CARTER
ANDREA JOHNSTON

Cover design and Formatting by Uplifting Designs
Editing by Karen L. of The Proof Is in the Reading, LLC
Cover Photo by Shutterstock

ISBN: 978-1-948852-16-6

Ear Candy

Marlena–

Romance Readers...
Am I right?
XOXO
ME Carter

Andrea Johnston ♡

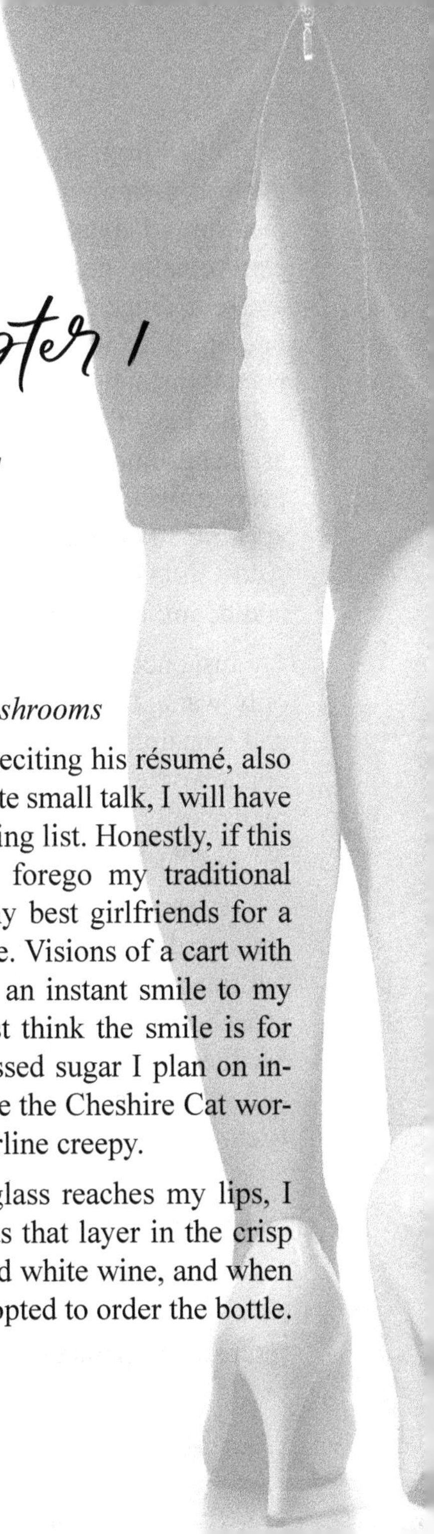

Chapter 1

Donna

Garlic

Dried Oregano

Oh . . . baby portobello mushrooms

By the time Rich finishes reciting his résumé, also known as his attempt at first date small talk, I will have officially completed my shopping list. Honestly, if this monologue continues, I may forego my traditional post-first-date cocktail with my best girlfriends for a rendezvous at the grocery store. Visions of a cart with ice cream and Ho-Hos brings an instant smile to my face. Unfortunately, Rich must think the smile is for him and not the box of processed sugar I plan on indulging in later tonight because the Cheshire Cat worthy grin he shoots me is borderline creepy.

Pausing before the wine glass reaches my lips, I inhale and savor hints of citrus that layer in the crisp Sauvignon Blanc. I love a good white wine, and when I realized Rich was a talker, I opted to order the bottle.

"More wine?"

Pulled from my thoughts, I peer over the rim of my glass at a smiling Rich. Handsome and debonair are the words I'd use to describe him in one of my novels. Actually, drop-dead gorgeous alpha male with an above average cock is how I'd really describe him in one of my books. That's what my audience would expect. Being a bestselling erotica romance author means I don't have the luxury of describing my leading men as "handsome" or "debonair." Nope, my audience expects a dirty talking billionaire with a strong sexual appetite and the occasional silk scarf for blindfolding. Add a little taboo—a ménage à trois or some BDSM—and boom: best seller.

Just once, I'd like to write about the sweet hero who only wants to show the woman he loves how special and amazing she is. I want to write the average blue-collar worker who meets the sweet small-town girl and realizes all he's ever wanted is standing in front of him. My agent calls that career suicide. I call it my life goal.

In response to Rich's question, I offer him a small smile and extend my glass for him to refill. When he's returning the bottle to the ice bucket, the server approaches our table to deliver our meals. A delicious Mediterranean chicken with roasted vegetables for me and a dripping blood steak and loaded baked potato for Rich.

As I pick up my fork and knife, I ask, "So, why corporate law?"

"The money, naturally. Growing up, I knew I wanted to be successful and not have to worry about my future so corporate seemed the most logical step."

And there you have it. He'll never be one of the sweet-talking men I dream of writing; he'll only be the billionaire alpha. Not that there's anything wrong with that. He's exactly my type on paper. Gorgeous. Rich. Successful. Arrogant. Taking the world by storm and determined to make his mark. The chemistry just isn't there. Or maybe it's because his inability to talk about anything other than himself seems to tip the scales to being a little *too* arrogant. Either way, I'm just not feeling this date, even if I'm not opposed to taking full advantage of the wonderful meal.

Nodding in response, I turn my attention to my chicken as Rich continues on with his reiteration of life as a corporate attorney. Lawyers like him are one of the reasons I left my previous life as an attorney behind. Being accountable to billable hours, demanding clients, and never seeing a sunset as I was chained to my desk was never going to make me happy.

Then, one bad breakup, a bottle of tequila, and a vivid imagination later, I hit publish on my first erotica romance novel. The big "FU" to my bosses and corporate life was using my real name. Donna Moreno isn't exactly the most creative name so whenever I'm asked if it's a pen name, I laugh. If I had known my good friend Adeline Snow then, I would have asked her to help me come up with a kick-ass pen name like hers.

As confident as I was when my book first released, when it began gaining buzz and popularity in social media, I started to worry. The fear that my bosses would catch wind of the release and I would suffer the consequences weighed on me like a hundred-pound boulder on my shoulders.

Imagining their bald heads turning various shades of red as they screamed at me, and ultimately fired me, kept me up every night. Then I hit the top one hundred of a major retailer and went to the store, purchased another bottle of tequila, and wrote the sequel. When the second book hit the top one hundred on release day, publishers began sniffing around. I weighed my options, read through their contract offers, and decided to throw caution to the wind. I rendered my resignation a few weeks later and never looked back.

Now, with twenty-three books under my belt, I live a comfortable life as a full-time author. And full-time single lady. The belief romance authors are having hours and hours of sex every day couldn't be further from the truth. The reality is, I spend days, okay, weeks, procrastinating. I watch a lot of mindless television, read a book a day, and possibly obsess over silly games on my phone instead of writing. Instead of pacing myself and finishing a project ahead of schedule, I fall down the darkest rabbit hole. Then, in the final weeks before my deadline, I spend my days in flannel pajama pants, forget to wash my hair, and live off a diet revolving around chocolate and potato chips.

By the time I take the last bite of my chicken, Rich has only made it a quarter of the way through his steak. I suppose failure to stop talking about one's self would make eating impossible. Perhaps that's why he's so svelte. Now, that's not a word you hear often. Svelte. Is it even appropriate to use when referring to a man? This is why I have editors, they always fix my faux pas and misuse, or overuse, of words. Except the word "cock." They encourage me to overuse that one.

"If I may," the server says as he extends his hand toward my empty plate.

"Yes, please. Thank you." I smile up at the young man in appreciation as he removes my plate. As he steps away, Rich says, "You can have mine as well."

"Should he box it up for you?" I ask.

"No thanks. I don't do leftovers." He doesn't "do" leftovers, but he'll waste food?

"How do you feel about a little dessert?" It's like the server read my mind.

Looking off into the distance, I spy the dessert cart. I saw the oversized slice of carrot cake when I walked in the restaurant. My mouth watered instantly. Regardless of how much sugary goodness may have welcomed me when I arrived, it isn't enough for me to endure another thirty minutes of this date. Turning my attention back to Rich, I see the look in his eye and realize he isn't thinking about the offered pastry or a cappuccino.

"I feel a little headache coming on; I should call it a night." Lies. I'm catching a ride share and taking my ass to the bar to meet my girlfriends.

"Probably the wine," he mutters. Rich doesn't bother to hide his frustration and it may be best for me to leave him to those feelings on his own. Excusing myself to the restroom, I grab my clutch and slip my phone out as I approach the ladies' room. I quickly open the app to order a ride-share. Nine minutes. Perfect. Next, I shoot a text to my best friend, Clara, giving her my ETA.

`Me: Twenty minutes or less.`

`Clara: I'm conflicted.`

`Me: Continue . . .`

`Clara: I mean, yay for girls' night but I wanted you to find love.`

`Me: Sorry to disappoint.`

`Me: WAIT! I did love my chicken.`

`Clara: You really are living your best life *insert sarcasm font* Give me a five-minute head's up so I can have the shots ready.`

And that is why she's my best friend. Or enabler.

I quickly handle my business, fluff my hair, and reapply my lipstick before returning to the dining room. As I approach the table, I see someone sitting in my chair. Across from my date.

Eating my carrot cake.

Granted, I never ordered it, but still. What kind of woman poaches another woman's dessert?

"Can I help you with something?" I ask politely as I approach.

Giving me the once over, the pretty redhead with overly pouty lips probably from too much Botox sneers at me. "We don't need anything, thank you. Although if you could get the check, that would be great. My husband and I are almost ready to leave."

"Your hus—" Not bothering to finish my question, I look over at Rich, whose eyes are as wide as saucers. Glaring at him, I don't mind making him sweat a little as he waits to see if I'll call him out. Not that I need to. His wife might be made of plastic, but she's not stupid. If my female instincts are correct, she knows she caught him red-handed, and she's enjoying making him squirm as much as I am.

Deciding this is one of those moments were women should be sticking together, I turn back to his wife. "Actually, I'm not your waitress, but I'll make sure to let the staff know you're ready to leave. The food here is amazing, if you ever dine here again may I suggest the steak. Rare. There's just something about a piece of meat dripping in its own juices. Plus the knives are really sharp."

Turning on my heel, I stalk out of the restaurant and to my waiting ride-share.

"Are you sure that was his wife? Maybe she's some psycho ex," my best friend says as she slides a shot glass toward me.

"Clara, she called him her husband. If she was an ex, don't you think he'd correct her? Plus the look on his face was pretty damning. I'm sure he's still wondering if she's going to shank him in his sleep tonight. Besides, I'm more pissed she got the dessert I'd been eyeing. I knew I should have ordered it."

Tossing back the shot of tequila and slipping the

lime between my teeth, I roll my eyes at Clara. She thinks it's so simple. Pull up an app, swipe left—or is it right? Maybe that's my problem. I must be swiping the wrong direction and keep ending up with the losers. Or assholes.

"Donna, you need to broaden your horizons. Give up on the suits and just date regular guys."

I scoff, feeling like a broken record. "I have a type. Tall, dark, handsome, successful. Why is that such a bad thing?"

For the last year I've been going on date after date thanks to an exclusive dating app for business professionals. The membership fee alone weeds out anyone whose income is less than mid to high six figures. My attraction to men in tailored suits who are driven by success has never wavered. I'm career driven, and while I want to meet a kind man with a good heart, I don't need the white picket fence and two point five kids.

"It's not a bad thing to have a type. Except your type also seems to be assholes and not good guys." Girlfriend has a point.

"Yeah well, I write assholes for a living. I guess I'm just living my best life. Or at least one my heroines would live."

"Maybe that's your problem," she suggests. "Maybe you need to write a different kind of guy. Throw it out into the universe and see if it comes back to you."

I look at her like she's lost her mind. "You think the reason my dating life isn't going well is because

I'm not putting the right kind of man into the universe? Have you been watching the Psychic Network again?"

Now it's her turn to scoff. "No." She looks down. "Maybe." I laugh as she continues. "That's not what this is about. I just think maybe you spend so much time focusing on a certain kind of man in your brain that it bleeds over into other areas of your life. Maybe if you shift your focus you'll see things a little differently. Men, in particular."

"Maybe," I say with a shrug. "At least I can try it. But if it works, my next book is going to be about an author who suddenly becomes independently wealthy and never has to work again."

"Oooh." Clara's eyes brighten. "Make sure you write in her beautiful best friend who finds the man of her dreams too, okay?"

"Done."

Clinking shot glasses with my friend, I lift it in front of me and toss it back. Clara is going to be sorely disappointed. If I've learned anything in the last year, it's that fiction does not meet reality.

Chapter 2

Todd

"I run my hands down her beautiful curves, tasting her as I move slowly down her body. She's the most beautiful creature I've ever seen, and finally, after all these months, she's mine.

"Her breath hitches as my tongue slides across her hip. My brain is singularly focused, wanting nothing more than to settle between her legs so I can taste her tight, wet …"

FLUSH!

Slamming my fist on the desk in frustration, I let out a shrill whistle before yelling, "Dammit Bill! We've talked about this! Flush on your own time! I have a book to narrate!"

He responds with an apologetic whistle of his own.

"Yeah, yeah," I grumble, trying to find a good starting point on my script now that I've lost my place. "You said that last time."

Making a mental note to add soundproofing insulation to the ceiling of my closet, also known as "The

Room Where the Magic Happens—Wink," I backtrack to the last paragraph and prepare to begin again.

Clearing my throat, I bring my lips to the microphone, and dropping my voice an octave to add maximum sexiness for this particular character, I speak.

"Her breath hitches as my tongue slides across her hip. My brain is singularly focused, wanting nothing more than to settle between her legs so I can taste her tight, wet …"

"Uh, Todd. I love you, marry me?" "Nope, sorry. Marrying Marge."

"Dammit. I was just getting to the good part," I growl, stopping the recording and picking up my phone now that it's alerted me of a call, via my favorite line from the '80s movie classic, *Mom and Dad Save the World.* My best friend, Aggi, hates that whole movie, which is why it's the perfect ringtone for her.

It also gives me a chance to plan how I want to answer when she calls. It's different every time. Deciding on the perfect accent, I press to connect. "If you want your book voiced soon, ya gonna need to stop intahrupting me."

"Not one of my characters has a Boston accent, Todd." I know she's rolling her eyes at me. I can hear it through the phone. "The only accent you should be using is a touch of Canadian."

"You have no imagination," I grumble, making a note on my script where I need to pick it up again.

"I have all the imagination," she retorts. "You're trying to bring *my* vision to life, remember?"

"It's called artist's interpretation."

"Please interpret less and narrate more."

"I'd love to, but I keep getting interrupted."

At this exact moment, Bill drops something on the floor above me. He's got nine hundred square feet up there. Why does he keep standing right above my closet?

Whistling again, I yell, "I'm working down here!"

"Good lord, Todd, was that necessary? I just went deaf from that whistle."

"Sorry." I'm not really sorry. Aggi likes to exaggerate. It's what makes her an amazing author and sometimes obnoxious friend.

No that's not right. I'm definitely the obnoxious friend in this relationship. Even I know that.

Growing up down the street from each other, Agnes Sylvester, Aggi to me and best-selling author Adeline Snow to the rest of the world, and I were practically raised as siblings. Her mom worked a lot, but with her brilliantly sharp mind was amazing at helping us with homework. My mom stayed home, but with her love of all things baked goods and soap operas, was awesome at keeping us out of trouble and nurtured.

It was like being raised in a lesbian household except with two houses and moms that weren't a couple. They actually didn't even like each other that much, just respected what they each brought to the table. It was kind of like that eighties show, *My Two Dads.* That show was how I learned that families come in all genders and sizes. I should see if it's on Netflix. I could go for some Paul Reiser comedy right about now.

No, Aggi and I weren't bullied for having two moms. We were bullied for being on the nerdier side. Not that either of us really cared. We had each other, our love of extreme sports, and the nursing staff at the hospital every time I fell off a skateboard and broke my arm.

Ah, how I long for the simplicity of childhood sometimes.

"You're not sorry," Aggi says, reminding me once again this is why she's my best friend. She gets me. "But I don't care. I was just checking in to see how it's going."

"Slow. If Bill would quit moving around upstairs!" I look up and say that part loudly for his benefit. Who knows if he hears me.

"Todd."

I know what's coming. "Don't say it."

"You can't stop me," she says quickly before continuing. "If you would add the soundproofing insulation to the ceiling like you were supposed to in the first place, you wouldn't have this problem."

"Listen Agnes—"

"And here we go," she mumbles.

Tossing my pen on my desk, I lean back in my chair, making myself comfortable for this next speech. "I bought this place so I could flip it. This is not a permanent situation. Living on the property saves me a pretty penny, and as soon as it's done, Bill and I are out of here. Therego—"

"Herego?"

"Thereby—"

"Ohmygod, you're so annoying—"

"Putting up more insulation is a waste of my time."

She pauses far longer than any normal person would. So much so, I have to look at the phone to make sure we haven't been disconnected.

Finally she speaks. "Are you finished yet?"

"Yes. My rant is over."

"You realize you would waste less time taking a staple gun to your ceiling, than the amount of time lost whistling for Bill to shut up and having to start over."

"Ah, my dear Agnes," I say haughtily, "one man's waste is another man's fertilizer."

A spraying sound comes through the phone and Aggi begins to choke.

It takes a few seconds, but finally she pulls herself together enough to berate me. "Dammit, Todd. I just spit water all over my laptop."

"Yet another reason why you should never argue with me."

"Okay." She sounds resolved. Interesting. "I quit. I shouldn't have asked."

Sighing, I decide to give her what she's asking for and ease what is sure to be a deadline of anxieties. For the sake of compromise and all that. "Relax, Ags. I'm almost finished. Bill isn't usually this loud. I think he ate some bad seafood or something and has the runs. The toilet has been flushing more than normal."

She groans again. "You are so inappropriate."

"You love it." She does. I know she does. She is as uptight and anxious as I am relaxed and going with the flow. We balance each other out in a weird sort of way. She's the yin to my yang. The Beavis to my Butthead. The Dumb to my Dumber. We wouldn't have it any other way. "When are you coming home for a visit, anyway? Your mother has been calling me to come change lightbulbs, which means she's lonely."

Aggi snorts, actually snorts a laugh, putting me on high alert. "No, it means you're a sucker for doing her busy work around the house. You know she has a book club at her house every Wednesday, right?"

My eyebrows shoot up slightly. "Since when does she read books?"

"Oh it's not the kind of books I write or the kind your mom reads. I'm sure it's something like the documented investigation notes on what really happened to the Titanic, or something. She also has a boyfriend."

"She what?!" I shake my head. "I can't believe she hoodwinked me into thinking she only needed some human contact. With a new boy toy she probably gets more contact than either one of us. You know those strong yet silent types."

"I'm going to ignore that you just went there. But I will say it's your own fault. My mother is sixty, not dead. She could probably run circles around both of us in the energy department."

Hmph. That's what I get for being a nice person. Swindled by the elderly-ish.

"But since you asked," Aggi continues, "I'm going to be in Portland in a couple weeks for a signing."

Sitting straight up in my chair, she has piqued my attention. "That's only five hours away."

"I know. It's a bit of a trek so don't even think about coming to see me. I just didn't want you to see it on social media or something and wonder why I didn't tell you. I'm actually kind of bummed to be going since Spencer can't come with me."

"So take me."

"What? Why would I take you?"

I second guess myself momentarily, but upon further introspection realize this is the best idea I've had since making Bill my building manager for when I'm away. Granted, he doesn't really manage anything, just makes sure no one breaks in to steal my circular saw, but it gives him purpose.

"You would take me because I'm your narrator." She makes a *hmm* sound and I know now is the time to put on some pressure. "I'm part of your book world now whether you like it or not, and I want to see what it's all about. Who are the readers I'm touching with my sweet words?"

"They're my sweet words, Todd."

"Who am I giving a verbal hug to in her time of need?"

"You're losing me. If you're going to be weird like

this, you can stay home."

Straightening in my chair, I prepare to beg. "Come on, Aggi. I can be your assistant."

"First, I have like four assistants already because my publisher insists I have plenty of help. Second, Hawk Weaver is my narrator."

"Then I'll just sit quietly and observe who the audience really is."

She goes quiet and I envision her biting her lip or picking at her fingernails while she thinks.

Lowering my voice to channel her popular narrator, I say, "You know you want to."

Finally she sighs. "Fine. But you have to make a choice. Are you going to out yourself as Hawk Weaver? Because that's going to give you a lot of attention and more people will come to my table."

Attention is something I don't really want. Neither of us want it, actually. Ever since Aggi started dating Spencer Garrison, skateboarding god and the star of every woman's wet dreams, her popularity has skyrocketed, which is crazy since she was so popular to begin with.

She's so hot now, it's been bleeding over to me as well. Once the audiobook I voiced for Aggi was released, I started getting messages from authors wanting to work with me. I still get them weekly. I turn them all down, though. This isn't a career for me. It's just something fun I do that incorporates my love of theater with my love of talking. Plus, it helps Aggi out. Other than that, I have no interest. But will I ever tell

Aggi that?

Nope. It's way too fun to make her squirm.

"Don't stress about that part, Ags. It'll give me a chance to try out a few different accents on my people."

She groans and murmurs, "This is going to end so badly."

Oh, but it's not. It's going to end so, so well. I can practically hear it already.

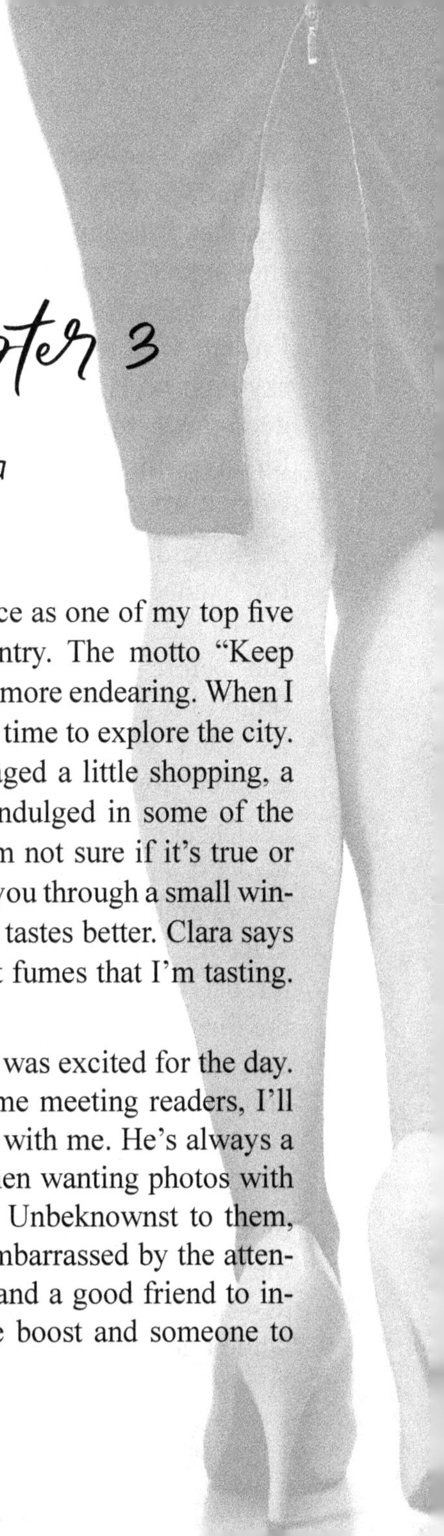

Chapter 3

Donna

Portland has secured its place as one of my top five favorite cities in the country. The motto "Keep Portland Weird" only makes it more endearing. When I arrived yesterday, I took some time to explore the city. Wandering the streets, I managed a little shopping, a lot of people watching, and indulged in some of the best street food of my life. I'm not sure if it's true or not, but I think food passed to you through a small window of a restaurant on wheels tastes better. Clara says it's the brake dust and exhaust fumes that I'm tasting. She's also a little dramatic.

Waking up this morning, I was excited for the day. Not only do I get to spend time meeting readers, I'll have one of my cover models with me. He's always a draw at these events, the women wanting photos with him while I sign their books. Unbeknownst to them, he's quite shy and is a little embarrassed by the attention. But, he's a professional and a good friend to indulge me when I need a little boost and someone to lean on.

One of my best author friends will also be here. On the surface, nobody would pair Adeline Snow and me together. When we stand side-by-side, the term "opposites attract" is never more evident. Adi is a petite brunette known for her retro style and clumsiness while I'm tall with too much blonde hair, tight skirts, and sky-high heels. She writes sports romances featuring good-guy heroes and spunky heroines, and I'm known for my arrogant bastards with dirty mouths and the women who fall to their knees before them.

Regardless, Adi is one of my closest friends, and I'm excited to hug her in person today instead of the virtual hugs and high fives I send her via text message. But, before I can do that, I need to drop off my table setup to my assistant and head to my appointment at the salon. When you have a mane of hair like I do, a good blowout before an event is a must.

Checking my purse for my phone, earbuds, and wallet, I slip my room key card into my back pocket before grabbing the handle of my cart of supplies and make my way to the signing room. As I exit the elevator, I see that although it's four hours before the event, the line of readers has begun to form. The hum of excitement is already filling the hallway and I know it's going to be a good day.

Walking into the large room, I smile and wave to friends also setting up their tables. I'm lucky that one of my reader group admins is local to the event and let me ship my books to her. She's also going to be my assistant today and offered to do my complete setup while I go to my hair appointment.

"Hi, Jennifer."

Popping up from behind the table, Jennifer smiles and stands. After a quick hug, she steps back and brushes the hair from her face, which is tinged pink with excitement. "I cannot believe Matthew Roberts is sitting with us today. I may die a thousand deaths."

"Only a thousand?" I tease.

"Don't tease me. Seriously, he's so dreamy. I cannot stand it."

Or maybe her cheeks are pink because she's horny. I better keep my eye on this one. No one wants to look over and see their assistant humping the cover models.

"Jennifer, he's just a guy. I mean, he's super-hot and all that, but he's just a guy."

Waving her hand dismissively, she giggles and mumbles under her breath as she moves to take the handle of my cart. "Don't worry about me, I'm sure I'll become a mute as soon as he gets here. You have an appointment, don't you?"

"I do. Are you sure you're okay setting up? I feel bad." I'm not used to someone doing this for me. I always do my own setup since I normally have a volunteer assistant and they aren't used to my preferences.

"I have pictures from your last few signings saved on my phone. I'll duplicate those and when you get here in a few hours, if you want to switch things we can. Don't worry. Now go get yourself more beautiful, if that's possible."

Reluctantly, I leave Jennifer to it. She has no idea how difficult this is for me. I might have a little control problem when it comes to my business. Having everything as perfect as possible is very important to me, and while I don't like to advertise my type A personality, it's also not exactly a secret.

I'm in the salon only a few minutes later, and as I settle into the seat waiting for the stylist, I pull my wireless earbuds from my purse and slip them into my ears. Tapping the icon for my audio book app, I bring up my current listen. Okay, it's technically the only book I've listened to for months. On a constant loop. What can I say? Hawk Weaver gives good audio.

As always, the story is beautifully written and each time I finish the book, I have a strong desire to be a better person. I want to find true love. Adeline writes some of the best sports romances out there and this one is no different. Except for the narrator.

Hawk Weaver has the kind of voice women fantasize whispering in their ear, speaking every dirty word imaginable, and making them climax without ever touching them. Hell, he could recite my grocery list, or the side effects of my antibiotics, and I'd probably need to change my panties. And, he's unattainable. He'll only work with Adi. Lucky bitch.

I mean that with the utmost love.

My new goal is to convince Adi to ask him to work with me. I'm already thinking of how my words will sound as he recites them. The thought alone has my heart racing.

The appointment takes longer than I expected but my hair is perfect. Lush and full of volume, there isn't a flyaway to be found. Picture perfect. Rushing from the salon, I return to my room to finish getting ready. I'm a firm believer in less is more when it comes to my makeup routine. This is mostly because I equally believe in a bold lip. It's one or the other for me. A simple cat eye and bold lip with my long hair perfectly styled have become my signature look. Well, along with a perfectly fitted dress.

Snatching a safety pin and ribbon from my travel sewing kit, I quickly attach it to the zipper of my dress before stepping into it. Shimmying the black frock up my body, I slip my arms through the sleeves and reach around to tug the ribbon up my back. Once the zipper is in place, I send a little thank you to online tutorials for getting yourself zipped into a dress when you're alone.

Leaning across the bathroom counter, I apply my deep crimson lipstick and step back to take in my appearance. Even I have to admit, I look pretty damn good today. Confidence has never been lacking, and today is no different.

Before I leave the room, I toss my lipstick and key card in my change purse. Time to shine and be the kickass romance author I am.

"You're sure you don't mind me doing this?" Jennifer asks for the fourth time in less than ten minutes.

"Girl, go. Meet all the authors, buy all the books. Just get me one of those lip balms from Adi before she runs out."

I've been trying to send Jennifer to get her own books signed by the other authors for the last thirty minutes. She's been reluctant to leave because my line has been pretty consistent. Matthew assured her he was capable of taking pictures and counting change for a while, so she could fangirl. He was sweet but had no idea how much she was freaking out as he talked to her, his hand on her shoulder. I'm pretty sure I heard her swoon. No humping, though. I call that a win.

We're in a bit of a lull in the signing right now so it's the perfect time for her to go explore and be a book nerd. I have to admit, I'm a little jealous. I've barely had ten minutes to chat with my friends. Although, I did get my required hug from Adi.

"Now that it's just us, tell me about what's new with you."

"You know, living the dream. Being a single woman living in the big city writing about all the dirty boys. It's a tough life."

"Uh huh. Don't bullshit me, Donna."

Matthew knows the struggles of dating as much as I do. Well, probably more considering how his life has changed in the last few years.

"Dating sucks. Well, the dating itself doesn't suck. I enjoy going out, meeting new people. It's the caliber of men I've been dating. Exclusivity my ass. I should probably freeze my account and wait for them to update their client list."

"Or, you could try not dating assholes. Like that guy over there." He points to Adi's table where her friend Todd is sitting. "What's wrong with him?"

Furrowing my brow, I look at him like he's lost his mind. "Todd? You think I should date *Todd*?" I met Adi's best friend briefly this morning. He was nice enough. Funny as all get out. But . . . no. "You realize he's wearing a shirt covered in heart shaped candies, right?"

"So?" Matthew says like he'd be caught dead in a shirt like that. "It is February. Maybe he just likes Valentine's Day?"

"The candies say, 'Eat Me'. It's creepy."

Matthew shrugs. "Maybe he's just affectionate."

I open my mouth to continue the debate, but we're interrupted by a trio of women who giggle as they approach us. Matthew turns on the charm, his green eyes sparkling, dimple popped for the full panty-melting smile he is known for, and his ink peeking out from under the sleeve of his T-shirt. The ladies stumble over their words as they thank me for writing such hot dirty talkers. When they ask Matthew to sign the chests of their "I like big books" shirts, I laugh as he pauses, making sure they really want his hands on their breasts. I love that he's so respectful and equally shy.

"Anyway," he says as the women walk away. I unscrew the cap of my water and lift the bottle to my mouth as he continues. "My point is not for you to date that particular Todd. But I think you need to change up your dating requirements."

"Why should I? Is it too much to ask to find a hot thirty-something successful man with a strong work ethic who is also looking for companionship and a healthy sex life?"

"I don't know that you can get all of that without him also being an asshole."

"You're not."

"That's because my focus isn't on being successful. I'm just a dad who has to feed his kid. I can turn on the charm when I need to, it's part of the job, but it doesn't mean women are throwing themselves at me."

Scoffing, I begin to tell him he could have any woman in this room if he wanted, but before I can, one of my favorite book bloggers walks up to the table. Carrie has been reviewing books for years, and she's become not only one of my biggest supporters but a great friend. She doesn't hold back when it comes to being honest about a book. I appreciate that about her. Plus, she's sweet as can be.

"I wondered if you were going to make it to my table. I saw you across the room and was starting to feel left out," I tease.

"You know I save the best for last. Besides, I had to hit all the preorders first. Since you insist on sending me signed books with each release, I don't have any to get from you."

Carrie's eyes glance to my left when she seems to only just notice Matthew. Following her gaze, I watch as he turns on the cover model charm.

"Hey, darlin' Are you having fun?"

Brows furrowed, Carrie replies, "It's fun as always. Anyway, Donna, I wanted to ask you about—"

"You wanna picture?" he interrupts.

"Um… no."

Bringing my hand to my mouth, I fake a yawn to hide the laugh that escapes. Shot down.

"Donna, I'll message you this week. I wanted to talk about a holiday giveaway idea I had. Talk to you later."

Matthew watches as Carrie walks away before turning to me. "See? It doesn't always work."

Laughing, I sit back in my seat and only half-listen to Matthew try to school me on the type of men I should be dating. Like Clara, he has this "put it out into the universe" concept. What I'd really like is to put Hawk Weaver and his voice out into my universe and see what happens.

How about that?

Chapter 4

Todd

I wasn't sure what to expect when I convinced Aggi to bring me to her signing, but it certainly wasn't this pandemonium.

Readers are supposed to be quiet, nerdy, and introverted. Maybe even in a constant state of library-approved quiet as they shuffle from place to place in their soft-soled shoes.

Oh how wrong I was. The entire day has been non-stop action which is the exact opposite of what I was hoping for on this mancation.

First, we got up at oh-dark-thirty to set up. Did Aggi come? No. No she didn't. Since she's the "celebrity" in this scenario, she had to take time to get all decked out in her Adeline Snow wear. It was a total copout if you ask me, but she got away with it.

And yes, I admit she looks hot. But it's giving me funny feelings in my loins that no one should have about the person who is practically their sibling.

shudder

Anyway, I got suckered into hauling boxes of books across the damn hotel before having my first cup of coffee. That's way too close to a workout for my liking. The last time I lifted weights was in high school gym class when I had to move a rogue plate off my foot after Aggi dropped it on my toe. Needless to say the school nurse had the hospital on speed dial after that incident in our weightlifting unit. I can still hear Aggi convincing me to take that ridiculous class, *"Take this class with me, Todd. It'll be an easy A."* Easy A my . . . *A-S-S.*

Which reminds me, I need to take some Valentine candy to the ER for Nurse Chilson. She always loves a good Godiva during a twelve-hour shift as I learned on my many trips to the ER over the years.

But hauling her shit wasn't the only surprise. When the doors finally opened a couple hours ago, signaling the beginning of this event, women ran, actually *ran* to get in Aggi's line. It was unreal.

It also cemented why I'm not a big reader. It's all too physically taxing for me. I prefer hobbies that don't mean dragging carts full of dead trees in circles around a room for eight hours. Even thinking about it sounds exhausting.

Since I'm already here, though, I've been taking advantage of my spare time by practicing different accents with the readers. I've also been pretending not to notice my BFF glaring at me from the corner of her eye. Clearly, she doesn't think my conversations are market research like I do. It's starting to wig me out that she can shoot daggers from her eyes at me at the exact same time she's smiling at someone else. The only other person who has ever been able to pull off that magic is my mother. Come to think of it, I bet they're in on this together.

As Aggi finishes with a customer, the line moves forward, and a cute brunette stops right in front of me. She's not paying much attention, too busy looking at the weird floor plan everyone seems to have. Some people even have them color coded. What is *that* about?

Watching her for a few moments, I make the determination that she's relatively normal compared to the room full of fangirls. She's the perfect guinea pig to try out my New York accent on.

When I clear my throat, she looks up at me. Now that I've got my eyes on my target, I open my mouth channeling Hawk Weaver's best interpretation of the *Friends* character, Joey Tribiani.

"How *you* doin'?" My head nods and eyebrows waggle for maximum effect.

She gives me a strangle look before saying, "I'm sorry, what?"

That wasn't quite the response I was going for. But since she asked, I might as well try again.

"I said 'How *you* doin'?'"

She cocks her head at me. "Is there something wrong with your face?"

"My . . . what?" Rubbing my hands all over my face, I try to figure out what she's talking about.

Pointing in the direction of her own forehead, she

adds, "It's just, your eyebrows did this weird thing when you were talking."

"What? No they didn't."

"Yes they did. They like, wiggled really weird."

I drop my head back and look at the ceiling in frustration. "That's called waggling my eyebrows. I'm sure you've read about it in one of Ag—Adeline's books."

"It looked like two caterpillars fighting."

"What?" I look over at Aggi who happens to be listening. She's way too amused by this conversation. "Oh look. The author is ready for your now," I deadpan. "Go get your book signed or something."

The brunette shrugs like she didn't just ruin all the dreams I had of nailing my Bronx accent today. Some people, I swear.

Sliding down into my chair I grumble to myself. "That didn't go as planned."

"Stop creeping out the readers," Aggi says to me after handing her latest novel to the woman who just crushed my soul and offended my eyebrows. "You're supposed to be helping me out."

"What are you talking about? I'm bringing in customers."

She snorts a laugh. What is it with her and the snorting lately?

"Uh, no. No you're not. See that guy over there?" She points to some hot stud at her friend Donna Moreno's table before taking a swig from her water bottle. I'm sure he's a Calvin Klein model or something.

Maybe Abercrombie. "*He's* bringing in customers."

"Well of course he is. When Ryan Cooper's doppelgänger shows up, everyone goes ape shit. I wouldn't mind licking his abs myself. He was quite the naked dancer in *Rough Night*."

"See what I mean? Your lack of filter is bringing those around you discomfort and a desire to run away."

"Sorry. Let me try being more alpha." Crossing my arms over my chest, I flex the new biceps that popped out after carrying all those books this morning. Dropping my voice an octave I give Mr. Personality the once-over. "I could take him."

Aggi rolls her eyes. "That's your idea of being alpha? Threatening to take him on?"

I throw my hands in the air with exasperation. "What do you expect from me? To whip it out and have a pissing contest? I know for a fact I can win that one, but I don't like embarrassing other men in public. It goes against part of the bro-code."

"I'm so afraid to find out how you know you could win that one."

"Donny Smithson challenged me to a piss off in the third grade. I peed way farther."

"Wait." She closes her eyes and crinkles her nose. "Is that when you got in trouble for peeing all over Mrs. Smithson's chihuahua?"

"It's not my fault Pepe ran into the stream."

Aggi facepalms herself, literally smacks herself across the face so hard she leaves a red mark. "This is why you can't get a date," she mumbles before turning her attention to the readers lining up in front of her table.

"Oh my gosh, you're dating Spencer Garrison," the short round woman with a bob gushes, making Aggie visibly uncomfortable. Serves her right. I bet that lady would love my New York accent. "Is he a good kisser? You can tell me."

Tuning out the lack of personal boundaries conversation, I glance around the room and find myself people watching again. Readers are absolutely fascinating creatures. All they talk about is plot lines and character issues. Someone even started crying when discussing the unexpected death of her favorite male lead.

At this point, I honestly don't know how many people in this room realize they read about fictional characters. It's definitely a fine line with this bunch.

Unsurprisingly, my eyes gravitate to the table directly across the way from us. Not to the Ryan Cooper look alike, but to the author whose books he cover models for. I met Donna briefly and she is quite impressive, to say the least. Not just in the way she presents herself, which, let's be honest, stirs more than just my loins. It's the way she carries herself. She looks like she could write a novel during the day, moderate a city council meeting in the evening, and run a marathon on the weekend for fun, and still find time for a mani/pedi.

That's not why I'm drawn to her, though. Something about the way her smile doesn't quite light up her eyes tells me that tough exterior is hiding an internal struggle of some sort.

Oh lord, I think, rolling my eyes at myself. I sound like I stepped out of one of Aggi's books. I need to hit the bar and order an Old Fashioned and a cigar, stat. Maybe I should see if Ryan Cooper wants to wrestle or shoot a gun with me or something else manly. Just not carrying books. I'm wiped from my workout this morning.

As I watch Donna though, I can't stop that niggling feeling that something else is going on. She looks put together in every way, but I don't believe it.

Shrugging my shoulders, I tear my gaze away. It's not like I'll ever get a chance to find out. Women like Donna don't flock to men like me. I'm just your average guy. Sure I'm a little on the taller side but other than that, I'm just a guy with brown hair, brown eyes, and a crooked nose that only a mother could love. That realization doesn't hurt my feelings as much as it keeps my expectations realistic.

I bet I could find a date in this sea of women if I practiced my cockney. That's what I should do. It's not like Aggi really needs me. I could go mingle and see if I can score myself a date.

Now where did that cute brunette go?

Chapter 5

Donna

Sleep.

I need sleep. Maybe I should give up some of the control in my business. If nothing else, perhaps I need to retain a full-time travel agent. I bet she wouldn't book my flights so I'm up, dressed, and waiting for a ride-share at four in the morning.

Four.

Nothing good happens at this hour. Is this the witching hour I've heard about? It sure as shit makes me feel *bitchy* that's for sure. In my twenties, I called this bedtime not wakey wakey time. Damn I'm crabby.

As much as I complain about the hour, I had a wonderful weekend. I almost sold out of my inventory and what was left, I traded with other authors. My personal collection of signed books is going to welcome these new beauties to the shelves and I can't wait to get them home. My readers never disappoint but this event was even more special. Not only did I finally put faces to the screen names I interact with on a regular basis, I was able to hug many I have become to think of as friends.

Spending the day with Matthew was a bonus, and I'm grateful for his patience with each of the readers who lost their minds at the sight of him and his damn dimples. Except for Carrie. Seeing her unimpressed with him made me love her even more. I'm sending her two of my books on the next release. She earned them.

The problem with sitting on a bench in front of this hotel in the dark is the inability to tell how long I've actually been here. Ten minutes feels like an hour. Tapping on my phone, I bring up the ride-share app for an update. What the heck? How has it gone from six minutes away to seventeen?

Sighing, I lean back against the cool window of the hotel and watch as others begin to file out of the building. Some are in pairs while there are a few single individuals milling around. I should offer to share my car with a few of the singles. It makes no sense for four of us to all have our own cars. Contemplating this idea, I spot Adeline and her sister-in-law-to-be, Kate, in the lobby. In true Adi fashion, she stumbles and then laughs as she rights her suitcase.

When the large doors slide open, Adi and Kate exit, not noticing me as they continue gabbing. I wait for a break in their conversation, so I can say good morning and see if they want to share a car, but the break never comes. Dear Lord, those two can talk. How do they breathe at the speed they're talking?

"I mean, I wanted to die. I just stood there. Like a mute, Adi. A mute. She must think I'm a complete loser."

"Kate, don't be ridiculous. You didn't look like a loser. A mute, maybe." Adi's tone is teasing, and I smile because as harsh as someone else may have thought she was being, my friend is too sweet to be cruel.

"Then, she had that hot-as-fuck model at her table. You had *Todd*, Adi. I mean, I love Todd. He's great. I'm not sure about his fashion choices but to each his own. For goodness sake, I'm married to a man who thinks socks with sandals is a good idea so I have no room to judge."

Covering my mouth to muffle my laugh, I continue to eavesdrop on the conversation. I saw Todd's shirt too, and while my first thought was he dressed himself in the dark, I wasn't really surprised. Adi is quirky so of course her closest friend would be too.

"The shirts are for a reason. The practice on his accents, however? I swear Todd does shit like that just to embarrass me. But enough about him. I know Donna is one of your favorite authors. I was *trying* to introduce you to help you with the whole super fangirl issue you have. She's just a person, like me."

Kate whips her head to look at Adi and I can't help but laugh at the look on her face. Horrified and maybe a little confused, she gasps. "She is not just a person. Donna Moreno is the epitome of kickass. She's crazy talented, runs what is going to be an empire, mark my words, and she has hair that any woman would kill for."

I kind of love Kate. So much so I can't let this go on much longer. As much as I want to have an empire, I'm just a woman who tells stories for a living.

"I can hear you, ya know," I say, standing from my spot on the bench.

Adi snorts and Kate gasps as I approach them.

"How long were you sitting there?" Adi asks, clearly amused. Kate on the other hand looks mortified.

Lighting up my phone, I look at the time before saying, "Too long. What is it with these ride-shares? First it was six minutes then it jumped to seventeen. It's been at least ten minutes since then and it still says seventeen."

I look up at the women before me, Adi is mid-yawn as she shrugs while Kate is staring at me, eyes wide and mouth slightly agape. I really should say something wise or endearing to help her relax a little. Instead, I'm going to enjoy being on a pedestal for a little longer. We all need an ego boost now and then.

"Did you have fun, Kate? I hope you were able to meet a lot of the other authors."

"I . . . uh—"

A car pulls up in front of us and I look to my left hoping it's a silver SUV with a driver named, Sal. It isn't. Turning my attention back to Kate and Adi, I open my mouth to ask if they want to share a car when I hear a group of women begin mumbling and one shriek. Goodness that was loud. Standing on my toes, I look around to see what the craziness is about. I don't see any models around but, I do hear the two words that set my heart racing immediately.

Hawk. Weaver.

Whipping my head around to where the women

stand, I barely hear Kate screech and Adi laugh when my hair whops her in the face. Did they say Hawk Weaver is here? Hawk *fucking* Weaver is here.

"Adeline Snow! Hawk Weaver is here?" I cock an eyebrow at her, which makes her look around the area, avoiding my gaze.

"Wha—"

"Don't 'what' me. Those women just said his name, and I think I heard one of their panties self-destruct. Where is he? I cannot believe you didn't tell me he was here." I stomp, yes actually stomp my foot like a petulant child, but this is important business. "You know I want to beg him to do my next book. I *need* him, Adi."

"I—"

Cutting her off, I wave my hand toward the SUV pulling up at the curb. "Of course my ride is here, sixteen minutes earlier than the app says. Ladies, please enjoy this ride-share on me. I'm going to find some ear candy."

Grabbing the handle of my suitcase, I toss my purse over my shoulder and hightail it back into the lobby to track down my man. Or narrator.

Semantics.

Twenty minutes of searching for a man you have no idea what he looks like is virtually impossible. Wrong. It's not virtually anything. It *is* impossible. You'd think in a hotel filled with primarily women it would be easy to find the man whose voice is going to make my books more popular than they already are. It's not.

The first three men I approached looked at me like I had three heads when I asked if they were Hawk. Of course two didn't speak English and the other, well he was English. I almost asked that guy for his number because, well, *English.*

Nothing. There is no Hawk Weaver and now I'm missing my flight. Jumping on the app to pay the one hundred-dollar rescheduling fee before the flight starts boarding, I see there isn't a seat available on my preferred airline for seven more hours. Sure, I could go to the airport and wait it out on standby or, I could try and convince the front desk to let me back into my room and let me sleep. Instead I'm sitting in the business center, my suitcase parked against the wall, and my current manuscript open. Taunting me.

I'm not blocked per se but I'm not feeling the story. Each word feels forced at this point. I could open a folder with another one of my works in progress and see if one talks to me. At this point, I'm not hopeful. I could start another new project, I suppose. Wouldn't my agent love that?

Lifting my coffee to my lips, I take a tentative sip, hoping it's cooled enough to eliminate third degree burns from my day as my phone and computer simultaneously alert me to an email. And then three more.

With a click of the mouse, I scroll through the emails coming through. Discounts for book swag, a reminder to pay my credit card bill, and a sale at my favorite store. A little online retail therapy sounds perfect, so I click on that email and drop a few shirts and a pair of skinny jeans into the shopping cart.

Not finding anything else to purchase, I finish my transaction before returning to my email. The last unopened email is from my agent. Scanning it, my heart sinks a little. Thirty days. I have thirty days to submit my next manuscript to her for submission to my publisher. She so kindly reminds me my commitment was for the first five chapters of book one in a new series.

A new series.

Another series about an uber rich man who wears expensive suits and fucks like a champ. Or, maybe I can submit something completely different. Would that be so bad?

With two clicks, I open a project I've been tinkering with for a year now. A sweet small-town romance. It's one of my personal favorite tropes: best friend's brother. I started writing this when I began this damn online dating process and secretly wished Clara had a long-lost brother I didn't know about. Life would be so much simpler if she did.

If I can convince my publisher to approve this book, it could open up a whole world of new readers. Sure, people might prefer to read mysteries or horror books. But romance readers are different. Most of them can read a friends-to-lovers book one day and get sucked into a dark romance the next, rounding out their weekend with a sports romance. As long as it has a love story, they're voracious readers. And if they have a voice like Hawk Weaver's narrating, they'll listen to a whole book in less than a day.

Hawk Weaver.

I'm still irritated I couldn't find him. I'm even more disappointed that Adeline didn't give me a hint as to who he is. I suppose it's not her story to tell, but still. She could have torn herself away from her friend Todd for two minutes to give me a heads up, so I could keep my ears peeled for his voice. I guess that's what happens when the elusive BFF shows up for his first signi—

Wait a minute.

It was Todd's first signing.

Where he spent the day at her table promoting her books and practicing his different accents.

Which I thought was just weird but—

"Son of a bitch!" I slam my fist down on the flimsy table, rattling all the monitors with the vibrations. "Todd is Hawk Weaver!"

Dammit, I should have known better and now I've missed my chance to talk to him face-to-face.

With a frustrated sigh, I switch back to the window with the email, re-reading the deadline before shutting down my computer and pulling up the ride-share app. I might as well head to the airport now. With this current bout of luck, I probably need to be ready for anything.

Clicking "submit," the app alerts me as to how long it'll take the SUV to get to me.

Six minutes.

Here we go again.

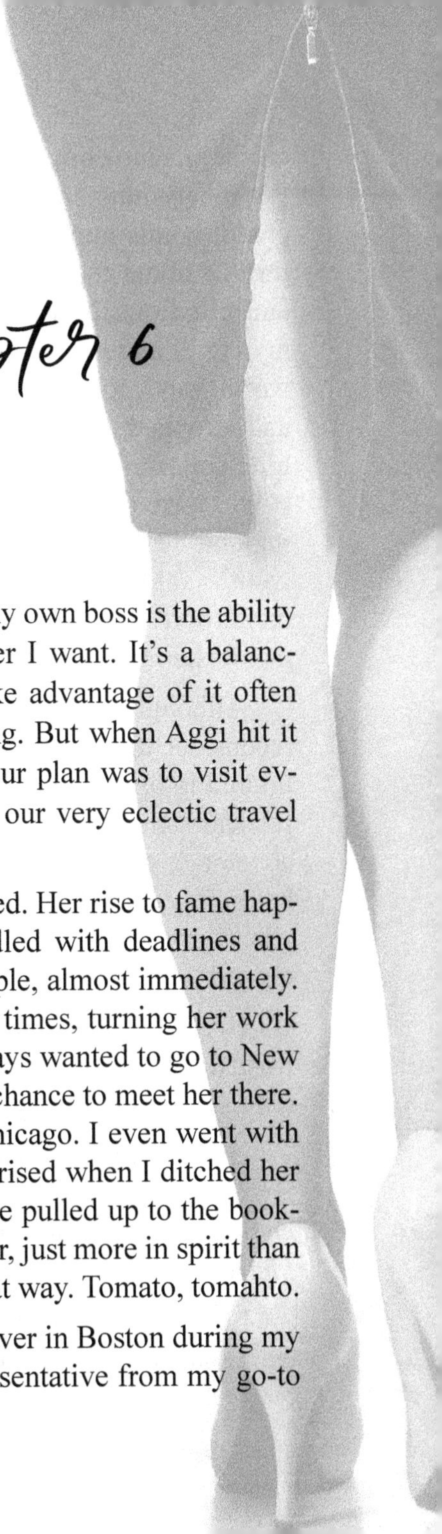

Chapter 6

Todd

One of the perks of being my own boss is the ability to take time off whenever I want. It's a balancing act, obviously. I can't take advantage of it often or I won't be the boss for long. But when Aggi hit it big, we promised to travel. Our plan was to visit every landmark and country on our very eclectic travel bucket list.

And then, it never happened. Her rise to fame happened quickly. She was saddled with deadlines and tours, scheduled by other people, almost immediately. I managed to tag along a few times, turning her work trip into my vacation. I'd always wanted to go to New York City, so I jumped at the chance to meet her there. Same with her first time in Chicago. I even went with her to Vegas. She wasn't surprised when I ditched her for the casinos the moment we pulled up to the bookstore. I was still supporting her, just more in spirit than in person. She didn't see it that way. Tomato, tomahto.

It was on a very long layover in Boston during my own business trip that a representative from my go-to airline tried to convince me to buy a club membership. For ninety-nine dollars a year I could get the card upgrade, bonus miles, and all the other perks. I wasn't thrilled about the cost, but I figured "what the hell?" and filled out the paperwork. After a quick check of my credit and income verification, they decided I was worth way more to them than originally anticipated and dropped my yearly membership fee to thirty-nine dollars. Only then did I sign on the bottom line. I would have done it for the hundred bucks, but wheeling-and-dealing is my gig. Besides, who doesn't love a comfortable couch and free wi-fi when you're stuck in the airport? I know I prefer it over the uncomfortable metal chairs at the gate.

Although, someone at the airlines should really reconsider their lounge policies. They'd probably be floored to find out I got a last-minute round-trip ticket for less than a hundred bucks *and* I'm about to take advantage of the unlimited pretzels and fancy coffee before my forty-five-minute flight. I don't think that's what they planned for when they increased my card rewards.

Giving me the once-over as I walk through the frosted glass door, the front desk attendant gives me a tight smile as I pull my identification out of my wallet.

Yeah, yeah. I know my shirt has pineapples wearing sunglasses on them, I think to myself as I hand over my information. You'd wear it too if you knew Marcy Metrick.

Logging me into the system, the attendant's facial expression changes. "Welcome, Mr. Chi . . . Chimi . . ."

I could let the poor girl continue to slaughter my name but instead put her out of her misery. "Chimolski."

Her shoulders relax, and she continues. "Yes, Chimolski. Welcome. You'll find fresh coffee and pastries in the lounge area and today's papers near the printers in the business center. As always, our men's locker rooms are fully stocked and available in case you need to"—her eyes give me the once over again—"change clothes."

Shoving my stuff into my wallet and my back pocket, I smile politely. "No thank you. I'm going to get some work done." No reason to be rude back. My mother always told me kindness was the most important thing to have when dealing with people. It hasn't proven her wrong yet.

Nodding, she turns back to her work while I head into the lounge area. First order of business: those pastries she mentioned. I can't very well check in with the office on an empty stomach. I left my team with three open houses this weekend, not including our regular clients. My brain needs to be powered by sugar if I'm going to keep track of all the updates.

Grabbing a cup of steaming hot caffeine, I doctor it with more sugar. Might as well go all out. Looking around for the pastries, my eye catches something else instead.

A tall, glamourous blonde who writes books for a living and looks better than any traveler should at—I glance at my watch—noon. Huh. Maybe everyone else shouldn't look so drab while traveling in the middle of the day.

The empty seat next to her looks comfortable and inviting. Plus, I know she smells good. Since I can't vouch for the guy sitting across the room who has that "I just got off a seventeen-hour flight" look, I'll take my chances next to Donna.

Straightening my shirt, because nothing is worse than crooked pineapples, I saunter over to her and clear my throat. With my best Hawk Weaver voice I ask, "Is this seat taken?"

She doesn't even look up from her laptop.

Well that's kind of rude.

But I'll give her the benefit of the doubt. Maybe she didn't hear me.

"Is this seat taken?" I say a little louder.

Still nothing. What the hell? I know she's awake. I can see her fingers moving. She rubs the tip of her nose and glances around, finally seeing me hover over her.

"Oh!" she gasps and pulls the earbuds out of her ears. "Sorry, I didn't hear you."

Glad to know she's not ignoring me, I lower my computer bag to the floor and my rear to the seat next to her. "I just got here. What are you doing in the lounge? I thought Aggi said you were heading out around the same time she was this morning."

Donna purses her plush lips and her face tinges with pink. Interesting. Donna Moreno is embarrassed about something. "Yeah. I . . . um . . . I missed my flight."

"Oh shit. That sucks. Have you been here all day?"

"Pretty much," she admits. "I decided standby was a better option than hanging out at the hotel for hours on end. At least here I can get some work done while I wait."

"That's why I don't mind flight delays. I always seem to get more done in this lounge than I do at home."

She furrows her brow in confusion. "How do you work . . . I mean . . . because of the noise and . . . oh geez."

Even though she's rubbing her temples, I'm the one who is confused now. "How do I work here? The same way you do. On my laptop. I work in real estate, I can do that from anywhere." Settling back into my seat, I cross my arms over my chest waiting for her to continue.

"Yeah, but how much can you really get done with all the background noise." She turns her head and nods towards the espresso machine whooshing and blowing steam.

I need more sugar. I have no idea what she's asking me.

"Because you're Hawk Weaver?" She says it like a question, lowering her voice so she won't be overheard. I'm not sure who Donna's worried about since the only other people in the room are Mr. International and the attendant who wouldn't give me the time of day if I hit on her.

Nodding in understanding, I tamp down my frustration. Aggi promised she'd keep my identity under wraps. If this gets out . . . there's no telling what those book nerds will do. I heard how they talked about all those audiobooks. I don't need that kind of sexual attention in my life. Besides, I'd never know if someone was dating me for me or for my sexy ass voice.

"You aren't supposed to know that, ya know."

Donna bites her lip. It's cute. Kind of makes me want to bite it too.

Dammit. I need to stop this side gig. Even my thoughts are going to the romance book fallback. Lip biting. How cliché. And hot.

"I accidentally figured it out," Donna admits, thwarting my plans to make Aggi pay for her betrayal. "I overheard someone say you were here and then Adi, sorry I guess we can actually call her Aggi, got all flustered when I asked her, and I started thinking about you practicing your accents during the signing. It wasn't hard to piece together."

"Hmm. And here I thought working on the different dialects would keep me incognito."

Donna makes a throaty sound when she laughs. I like it. "Looks like things didn't go as planned."

"It appears not."

Flipping open my laptop I connect to the internet.

"But to answer your question and since you're already a super spy who will probably figure it out anyway, no, I don't work on the narration here. That's just a side gig."

"You're not trying to make a career out of it?"

"Nope. I started doing it because I was bored and needed a hobby."

"Wait," she holds her hand up to stop me. "You became the most sought-after narrator in the indie book community to pass the time," she deadpans.

I move my head back and forth indecisively. "That and I figured I might get a date or two out of it. Who can resist this sexy voice?"

Donna laughs heartily. "That's awesome. Has it worked so far?"

"Not even close."

This time, she bellows with laughter. "That's so sad."

I shrug. "I know; I've got a face for radio. But someday, mark my words, some woman is going to close her eyes, hear me talk, and decide I'm the one for her. Or she'll be visually impaired, and it won't matter anyway."

"Ohmygod you're so bad!" she cries out in amusement. "So self-depreciating."

"It's not self-depreciating. It's finding the fun in a normal situation. Keeps life simple."

"I could use some simplicity in my life," she grumbles, turning back to her computer.

"Let me guess. Writer's block?"

She shakes her head.

"Lagging sales?"

"Still nope."

"Copyright infringements?"

She looks at me and smiles. "You sure do have the lingo down. Aggi has taught you well."

"Hey, if you're gonna be a good business man, you better know business." Bumping her shoulder with mine, I continue. "But really, what's the issue?"

She sighs and lightly taps her fingernails on the keyboard, not typing anything as much as fidgeting. "I want to write something different than my normal stuff. I'm not bored. I just want to stretch my creativity a bit."

"So do it."

"It's not that easy."

"Why not? You have a story in your head. You put it on paper. The end."

She gives me an incredulous look, and I have a bad feeling I'm going to get the same lecture Aggi has given me more times than I can count.

"You do realize it's kind of insulting to tell an author their job is simple, right? It takes time and energy to write a book. Not everyone can do it."

Yep, I was right. Different words. Same lecture.

"Believe me. Your good friend *Adeline* tells me that all the time. Usually she follows up with a really bad attempt at punching me in the shoulder. She has a permanent bruise on her knuckles to prove it."

Donna shakes her head at me. "It's like talking to a standup comedian with all these one liners."

"And my mission to bring laughter to the world is

accomplished!" I raise my hands in victory, eliciting an evil glare from the attendant. Quickly, I put my arms down. I can't afford to be kicked out of here. I haven't gotten my free pastry yet. "Since no one around here has a sense of humor, let me rephrase. Pick a project and just do it. What's it gonna hurt?"

She looks at me for just a second then gets a resolved look on her face. Closing her laptop, she turns to face me, determination written all over her. Suddenly I feel like a caged animal and she's on the prowl. I'm not sure if I'm nervous or excited about where this could lead, but I don't have to wait long to find out.

"I want you as my narrator."

I stare blankly at her. Damn my super sexy voice and how many women want it. I bet no one ever solicits the guy who voices Mickey Mouse for their audiobooks.

"You blew me away with *Effective Edge,*" she continues. "Your tone. Your delivery. The sexy growl thing you do during the sex scenes."

My eyebrows shoot up in amusement. "You think my growl is sexy?"

"So sexy." Her eyes practically roll to the back of her head as she thinks about it. This conversation has suddenly gone from uncomfortable to super horny. Me likey.

"I want that for my books, Todd. I know you only work with Aggi, but will you at least consider it?"

"No."

She reels back like I've audibly slapped her. I almost feel bad, except I'm still enjoying that she thinks my growl is sexy. That could be a country song.

"It's not that I don't want to. I just don't have time."

"But you said you were bored and needed a project to master."

"Yes, but I also have a job. A business. I narrate Aggi's books, but that's once every six months with her current publishing schedule. If I added any more projects, I wouldn't have time for my actual work. And let's face it, once word got out that I took on a new author, I'd have to switch careers, and I just got my new business cards. Five hundred cards can't go to waste. Those trees would have died for nothing."

Donna laughs, but it doesn't reach her eyes. I feel kind of bad when she turns back around in her chair and opens her laptop again. But not bad enough to say yes.

There's so much on my plate, if I can't say no sometimes, other things will be half-assed. There are too many people counting on me.

Still, as we silently work next to each other, waiting for our flights to be called, my brain keeps trying to figure out the timelines of the various projects I'm balancing. If I could figure out a way to work Donna in I would. Even if it was only to see that sexy eye roll again.

Chapter 7

Donna

Lying on my couch, staring at my ceiling, I'm doing my best Cher impression. Not literally. I'm fit, but only so many divas can make a black see-thru leotard and fishnets work. No, mine is more in the mantra, "If I Could Turn Back Time." I'd start small with last month in Portland. I would have talked to Todd sooner and convinced him to work with me on my next audiobook. I'm sure if we had more time to talk than the hour in the airline lounge, I could have used my powers of persuasion to convince him. And no, by powers I don't mean boobs. Okay, maybe I mean boobs.

Then I would have gone back to my twenty-sixth birthday and not kissed Ron on the dance floor. That kiss led to two years of chaos. He was a hell of a kisser but a shitty boyfriend. I digress.

As the narrator repeats the final words to the book, I smile and let out a long breath. It never gets old. Seeing my words on the page is one thing but hearing them spoken, the emotion surrounding me, enveloping like a warm embrace. I love it. He may not be Hawk Weaver, or Todd, but Alex Kingsford is pretty fucking perfect. He does alpha asshole billionaire sex god like nobody else. I'll miss him when I finally get Todd on board.

Rising from my spot on the couch, I click off the audio sample on my phone and grab my laptop. My email to my agent is open with the notes I painstakingly made from the first half of the book. I really want her to be on board with this idea, so I've gone into more detail than normal, really driving the point home. Adding a few additional points of reference and suggestions, I click send and close the lid of my laptop.

Now what?

Writing. I am supposed to be writing. I made a deal with my assistant that I wouldn't be on social media for three solid days. Sure, my commitment and promise was to write for those three days. In theory I could have almost half a book done in those three days. Or . . . I could watch cat videos and a few tutorials on how to properly curl my hair with a flat iron.

Hello my good friend, procrastination.

Instead of falling down the rabbit hole of mindless internet searches and videos, I walk to the kitchen and pull open the refrigerator door. Cocking my head from side to side, I take a moment to admire my bounty of fresh produce, bottles of my favorite wine, and the to-go containers from my leftovers from last night's disaster of a dinner.

When he told me his name was Rico, I should have known my date would think he was "suave." He's not. He's just like all the other power-hungry bozos I keep meeting—looking for a trophy wife and a good time, not necessarily with the same person. It's exhausting. But at least I'm getting good at picking the restaurants. My dates might be getting worse, but my leftovers are getting better.

Too bad I'm not in the mood to revisit the leftover lasagna right now. I should make myself a gigantic salad with a homemade citrus dressing. Low calorie and delicious. Or . . . yep, there's a better choice. I grab the carton of milk, take the box of my favorite sugary cereal from the pantry, and pour myself a huge bowl of bad carbs. Dinner of champions, folks.

As I shovel in spoonful after spoonful of sugary goodness into my mouth, I pick up my phone and scroll my social media accounts. If I don't go into my messenger or actually comment on any posts, nobody will know I was here.

I lurk in a few author groups I frequent and see that, once again, it's a different day yet the same story in the life of an author. Drama, chaos, and a sense of confusion on where our industry is headed. I'll tell you all where my future is headed—to another bowl of cereal. I'll just add an extra thirty minutes on the treadmill tomorrow to counteract the calories.

Taking my bowl with me, I return to the couch and grab the remote control to begin flipping through the channels. Stopping on one of my favorite romantic comedies, I settle in to watch my favorite kind of romance. The wallflower who believes nobody will see her for who she is. The woman who is destined to be passed over for the more beautiful, much more successful, and less compatible beauties until the hero sees her for who she is. And falls in love.

Simple, sweet, and approachable romance. It's cheesy at its finest and it's what I love—a simple, heartfelt love story without all the unnecessary angst and drama from traumatic childhoods and broken lives. It is not at all what I write but it is what I believe is possible. And let's face it, it's far more likely that a sweet girl with a kind heart will find love with a chef, or heck, even a prince, than it is with the smoking hot alpha male who has more money than he'll ever spend in a lifetime and meets his match by accident.

At about the halfway point of the movie, my phone chimes with a text message. Picking up my phone, I tap the icon and see it's Aggi.

`Aggi: I think I'm blocked.`

I quickly tap out a response.

`Me: I doubt that.`

`Aggi: I've typed "Stuff happens and it's funny."`

`Me: I stand corrected.`

My phone rings and Aggi's name appears on the screen. Answering, I sigh into the phone instead of greeting her with words.

"Oh no! You too? We're both blocked?" The anxiety in her voice sends panic through my veins. I hate the word "blocked." Mostly because unblocking is exhausting so I try not to say the word.

"I prefer paused instead of blocked."

"Donna, you are a genius. We aren't blocked, we

are paused. Yes!"

Laughing, I grab my remote and actually pause the movie I'm watching. "I'm not blocked or paused, I'm just uninspired. What's your story?"

"I'm not blocked either. I'm restless. I'm at that pivotal part in the story where I can either pick up the heat or I can continue with the slow burn. Spencer wants me to push my deadline and go with him to Los Angeles for a few weeks. Relax at his, sorry, *our* place and reset my mind."

"If only it were that easy," I murmur. "Although, I could go for a few days of relaxation. Maybe I'd know what to do with my story. You may be at a pivotal point in yours but I'm not sure which direction to go with mine."

"Why? Usually you have your plot lines nailed down before you start. I've never met anyone who can outline like you can."

She's not wrong. Years of drafting motions and briefs as an attorney still bleeds over a bit into my new career from time to time. I can get an idea and just run with it like everyone else. But when I have more voices talking to me than hours in the day to tell their story, a good, solid, detailed outline gives me the ability to get things done remarkably quickly.

Normally.

Resting my head against the couch cushion, I sigh again. "I have an outline in the can that I could use, I just don't know that I want to. The creative in me kind of wants to break out of the mold and do something completely different."

"So why don't you?"

"That's where the pause comes in. Maybe I'm just psyching myself out. Fear of failure and all that jazz."

Aggi snickers. "I love that movie." And now she's belting out the theme to the musical Chicago in my ear.

"Okay, okay!" I yell, making her stop while she giggles. "I know. I'm so punny."

She giggles again. "I'm going to ignore your sense of humor right now, because I may have an idea that can help us both."

I know Aggi. Her ideas are either exactly what the doctor ordered or they're slightly ridiculous. "Okay, hit me with this grand idea."

"What if we went away for a few days. Just us. We take our laptops and write non-stop. Of course, we'll stop for food and wine, but other than that we just write. I'll find us somewhere peaceful and serene. A place we can take walks if we need to clear our heads and big comfy beds to nap."

"Now you're speaking my language. Wine and naps. Is there food at this wonderland you speak of?"

"Yes." Exasperation is evident in her tone, as if she's appalled I think she'd forget. This from the woman who was just singing showtunes in my ear. "I'll make sure the fridge is stocked with cheese and crackers. What do you say? I think if I'm away without any distractions, specifically my sexy-as-hell fiancé, I can finish this book and meet Spencer in L.A."

Contemplating her proposal, I sit quiet for a few beats. A trip somewhere, anywhere, sounds fantastic. I'm going stir crazy here and not making any progress with my book. Or books. I haven't decided which series I'm going to focus on. My gut says go with the moneymaker, but my heart wants me to push my limits. To challenge myself, and my readers, with something different.

"Take the risk."

"What risk? Donna, does that mean yes?"

"Yep. I think it does. But, where will we go? I think I need minimal communication opportunities. You know how easily distracted I can get with cat videos."

"Mm-hmm. You're the worst with that. Okay, I'm going to handle it all. Wait for my text with the information."

Rising from the couch, I walk down the hall to my bedroom and pull my suitcase from its perch in my closet. As I slide open the zipper, I offer Aggi the appropriate "yep" or "nope" in response to her questions before I realize I never unpacked from Portland. I seriously need a handler.

And then one word brings me right back to the conversation.

"Wait, did you say snow?" She can't be serious.

"Yep. Nothing is better than the beauty of the mountains in winter. Okay, pull out your gloves and scarves, lady. We're going to the mountains!"

Before I can offer a response, Aggi disconnects the phone and I throw myself on the bed. Relaxation is white sandy beaches with a cabana boy fanning me, not snow and falling on my ass in the ice.

I really should have paid more attention to her when she was rattling off her destination options.

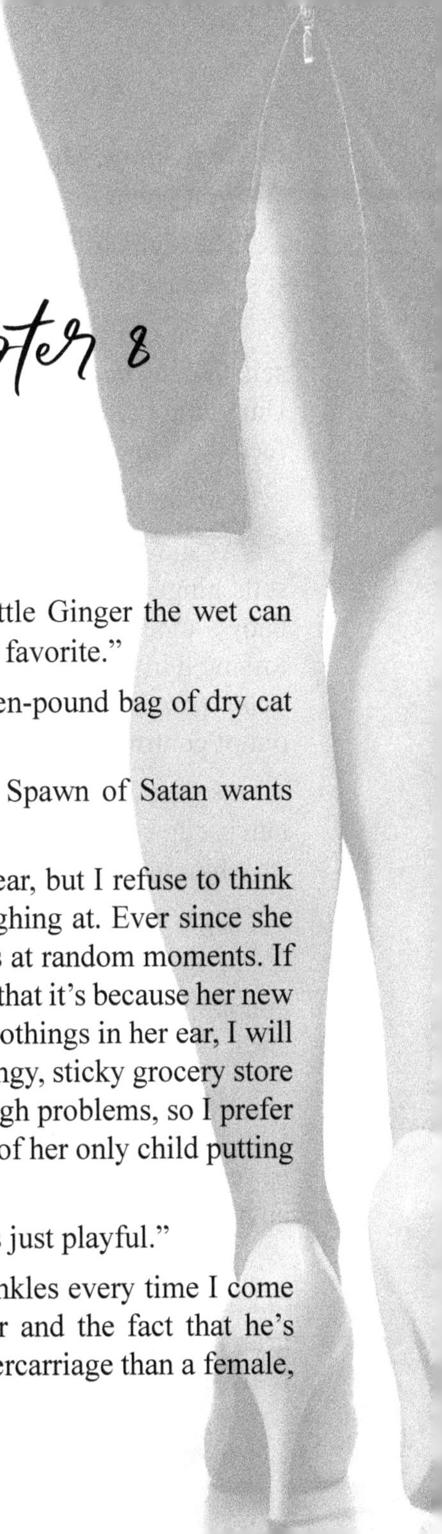

Chapter 8

Todd

"Now you know to get little Ginger the wet can food, right? Tuna is her favorite."

I roll my eyes and toss a ten-pound bag of dry cat food in my cart.

"Yes, mother. I know the Spawn of Satan wants wet food."

She giggles lightly in my ear, but I refuse to think too hard about what she's laughing at. Ever since she remarried last year she giggles at random moments. If I so much as entertain the idea that it's because her new husband is whispering sweet nothings in her ear, I will toss my cookies all over the dingy, sticky grocery store floor. Whoever mops has enough problems, so I prefer to believe it's the witty charm of her only child putting her in high spirits.

"Stop that, Todd. Ginger is just playful."

"He hisses and bites my ankles every time I come over. He doesn't have red fur and the fact that he's packing more parts in his undercarriage than a female,

I have to know, Mom, why did you name him Ginger? Are you going for irony since he has white fur?"

She sighs in exasperation. "We've gone over this. It's because he loves eating the ginger from my sushi."

"That can't be good for him," I mutter, eyeing the self-feeding bowl on the top shelf. If my mother thinks I'm going to her house every day for the next week to feed the demon, she has another thing coming.

"Actually, it's extremely beneficial to cats."

As she drones on about how her holistic vet's office sells ginger capsules so she can sprinkle it in her fur baby's food, I climb up the shelf and grab the feeder, tossing it in the cart. Let's see how Beelzebub likes not being pampered for a while. Seriously, my mother is out of control.

"So anyway, half a can of wet food twice a day and half a cup of dry food in the morning. If you want to give him milk, give it sparingly."

Right. Because I'm going to give her cat milk.

"I know, Mom. You left the instructions on the counter. In triplicate and translated in Spanish just in case."

Mom giggles. Again. Gross. "No I did not, you silly boy. I just haven't gone out of town for this long in years. Maybe ever. I want to make sure I don't miss anything."

"You're going to miss your flight if you don't stop talking my ear off." Pushing the cart down the aisle, I grab an extra litter box. It's good for him to have options since I'll be checking on him all of twice.

"Oh! You're right. I've got to run. I love you, honey."

Smiling, I melt back into our very comfortable mother-son relationship. It was just us and Aggi growing up so we're closer than the average family. "I love you too, Mom. Have fun on your cruise. Don't drink and fall over the balcony."

"Todd! You naughty kid! Don't put those thoughts in my head! You know I'm nervous already."

Laughing, I take a few more seconds to calm her down and say our goodbyes. Just as I press the red button to end our call, Aggi's dramatic ring tone indicates she's the next person I have to talk to.

Exasperated, I throw out my hands and say to no one in particular, "Why am I so popular today?" Looking down, I find a small child staring at me. "What? It's both a blessing and a curse."

He just stares blankly, then shrugs and walks away as I swipe to connect the call.

"What up, Ags?"

"Todd!" She sounds out of breath.

"That's my name. Don't wear it out."

"Har, har." She grunts through the phone and I immediately run through my mental calendar trying to remember if Spencer is out of town or if he's the one making her breathe heavy. I'm praying it's the former. I was just traumatized by my mother's giggling. I can only take so much. "I need your help."

"I'm going to assume you need someone with big,

strong muscles to come help you with some project in your apartment."

She snorts a laugh and then grunts again, like she's moving something heavy. Again, I hope it's not Spencer. "If I needed a man with muscle I'd call Jake in maintenance."

"Well that was rude."

"It's not rude if it's fact."

"You're not making a good case for me to help you, Ags."

"You're right. Also, I'm in a rush so I'll get to the point."

This is the moment in any conversation with my best friend that I know I'm about to be suckered into something. If she's rushing when she needs help, it won't matter what the task is. It won't matter what my answer is. I'll still end up doing it because Aggi won't be there to find another victim—er—helper.

"I'm going to L.A."

"Great!" I exclaim without missing a beat. "What time are we leaving? Do I need a ticket, or do you have one for me already?"

"You're not coming with me this time, Todd."

"Still rude," I mutter.

"Spencer hurt his bum knee again. I don't know how bad, but I need to get to L.A. before he goes in for surgery."

That's not good. I know Spencer is getting close to retirement, but that's the second time he's sustained an injury in just over a year. Retirement may find him if it's bad enough.

"So do you need a ride to the airport or something?" I offer because I'm a good friend like that.

"No, I need you to let Donna into the cabin."

"What?" I roll my eyes dramatically even though she can't see it. Owning the character is important, no matter who is watching. "I have so much to do."

Truthfully, I have no problem letting Donna into the cabin. She's nice, and we enjoyed chatting it up at the airport. But if I'm going to deal with my mother's possessed feline, I need to find pleasure in the little things. Giving Aggi a run for her money fits the bill.

"You have a team of ten people under you, Todd. You have jack shit to do," she argues.

"That's beside the point."

"It's totally the point."

"Don't judge me, Agnes. You don't know my life."

"I know your entire life."

She's right. She does. And frankly, I have no other points to make in this argument so I'm going to chalk it up to practice for next time and concede. "Why is Donna coming here anyway?"

Aggi grunts again, only now I realize it's because she's lugging her suitcase around the room. Chances are, she forgot to unpack it before putting it away after her last trip so it weighs a zillion pounds. "She's writing a sweet romance and needs to get to a sweet location to find some inspiration."

"Oh good. She decided to go for it."

Pushing my cart, I stand in line behind that weird kid and his mother again. He's creepy, just staring at me like he's auditioning for the next lead in a *Children of the Corn* remake. I bet he and Ginger would get along great, but he's got another thing coming if he thinks he's going to intimidate me. I once won the staredown contest in seventh grade. I had to use Visine for two weeks afterwards because my eyeballs were dehydrated. But this little shit doesn't know that. He has no idea the extremes I'll go to win.

"Well, she's not one hundred percent on board yet. That's why I offered her a cabin getaway. A change of scenery will probably do her creative brain some good."

The staredown with creepy boy continues. His eyes twitch ever so slightly. I narrow mine. We move a step forward in the line.

"Wait," Aggi interrupts the contest. Fortunately, I don't even flinch. I am *that* good. "How do you know what Donna has been working on?"

"You're not the only one who knows things, Ags. She's my friend too."

"Really," she deadpans. "What's her phone number?"

"I don't have to know how to reach someone to know there is a special connection." I'm full of shit. We both know it. But right now my only goal is to win, no matter who I'm competing against. That mindset is the only way I'm going to take down this beady eyed little punk. "Don't you have a plane to catch?"

"Crap. Yes." Aggi's breathing gets heavy again like she's racing around her place. "Thank you, thank you for letting Donna in. And don't forget to stock it with wine and snacks. And make sure it's clean since Frida quit the cleaning service."

"What?" I bellow in shock, looking away from my competitor. As soon as I realize what I've done I glance back over to see him smirking at his victory. Dammit! I must have blinked. That's what I get for not keeping tabs on the cleaning staff. "What do you mean Frida quit?"

"Don't you ever check your emails?"

"It's so impersonal. I prefer a phone call or face to face conversation." I complain, turning my cart around and heading to the alcohol section. I knew the second I answered her call I was being screwed into something annoying. Not only do I have to stock supplies, I have to clean the toilets too. Damn Aggi and her being the best friend I've ever had and who I would do anything for!

"Well, that's not the way the world works, but I'm not going to argue with you."

"Says the woman who has only just purchased her first smart phone."

"I'm ignoring you. Plus, I have a plane to catch in—shit—less than two hours. I'll text you from the airport. Thank you, love you!"

She hangs up before I can properly say goodbye or berate her for tricking me into doing her dirty work once again.

It doesn't take long to find what I need in the small market. There's not much variety so it's basically a coin toss. Red or white wine? Ritz crackers or saltines? Cheddar cheese or . . . actually there are a ton of cheese options. Small town living has come a long way from when I was a kid and real cheddar or Velveeta were the only options. I'm able to pick up a . . . Drunken Hooligan—what the hell kind of cheese name is this? Whatever, it sounds fancy. Sold. And some mozzarella *and* gouda just to play it safe.

A few other staples and the cleaning supplies I may or may not need round out my purchases for the day. By the time I make it up to the counter, Poltergeist is gone and it's just me and the cashier.

"Hey Marcy," I say politely as I unload well over fifteen items onto the belt. If anyone asks why I'm in the fast checkout lane, I'm blaming Aggi for springing her latest idea on me and shaking me to my core.

"How's it going, Todd?" Marcy responds, carefully scanning each item. I've never quite understood why they have her in the fast lane. She's the slowest cashier ever. Maybe management thinks the fewer items for her to scan the better.

"It's going. Aggi's headed out of town, so I'm going over to the cabin to let her friend in."

Marcy nods and continues her work, chewing on her bottom lip. We do this song and dance often, so I give her time to pull together her nerves. It takes a few more silent minutes, but finally she blurts it out.

"I designed some new shirts."

I respond appropriately, eyes wide with false excitement. It makes Marcy feel good, and after everything she's been through, a little support won't hurt. "Yeah? You didn't happen to bring one in my size, did you?"

She nods. "Your total is twenty-seven dollars and fourteen cents." She doesn't bother to bag my items as she reaches under the counter. "The shirt is an additional twenty-five. But it's good quality cotton and handmade by me."

Peeling three tens from my wallet for the shirt, I hand them over. "I don't doubt you at all. The handmade part is why I'm your best customer."

I'm lying through my teeth, but she's beaming, so I don't care. Marcy's shirts are ugly as sin. There is no denying it. But I know the cash I'm handing over to her will likely feed her child for the next week or keep her lights from being shut off, so I don't care. It's not like fashion is that important to me. Helping out a former schoolmate who is going through a rough financial time is more important. That's why I wear her ugly shirts proudly. Because Marcy is working hard to survive, and when anyone in town sees her creation on my back, it's a reminder to them to not forget Marcy and her son. And we don't.

She takes the money from me carefully, opening up the money bag behind the counter and situating the bills before handing me a five. All this goes down while I'm using the credit card machine to swipe for my groceries and bagging things myself. If it was any other cashier, I might be upset, but at least this way I know the wine bottle isn't going on top of the bread. Marcy is super book smart but a professional grocery bagger, she is not.

Handing me a plastic grocery bag with my shirt in it, Marcy thanks me for my business. Not sure if she means my grocery business or my buying a shirt, but it's no matter. I'll be back for both again anyway.

I step outside the door and around the corner, stopping to pull open the bag. Call me a glutton for punishment, but I'm really curious what kind of atrocity I'll be wearing now.

Pulling the clothing out of the bag, I groan.

Cats. It's a shirt covered in cats. And they look just like my mother's favorite feline.

Aggi is never going to let me live this one down. I have a bad feeling Ginger never is either.

Chapter 9

Donna

This is by far the most ridiculous thing I've done for a book. Okay, untrue. I did wear that latex bodysuit for an entire day once so my character could describe the experience correctly. And then I paid the price. If I were asked to share a piece of wisdom with the world, it would easily be to research the proper ways to wear latex. Specifically, removing said latex. Thinking of the process makes my skin crawl. Which is saying a lot since it felt like my skin was peeling off that day.

I digress.

The most impulsive thing I've ever done for a book is more accurate. Packing for a trip to a small town I've never heard of for inspiration is right up there on the ridiculous scale. I've never needed to step out of my normal process, in particular, my office or off my couch, in order to embrace a storyline. But, Aggi was very convincing, and I could go for a girl's weekend regardless.

Since I'm more of a fun-in-the-sun kind of gal, I've

had to spend a little time online shopping for warmer clothes. I didn't realize how much room some of this stuff would take up in my suitcase. Tossed aside is my favorite mid-size suitcase and in its place is the large monstrosity I save for signings. This baby is usually stuffed full of swag, extra books, and the seventeen outfits I take with me for a three-day trip.

Today, instead of an assortment of pencil skirts, my suitcase holds snow pants, a pair of fuzzy waterproof boots, and half a dozen sweaters. Of course, I've tossed in my favorite pajamas and my fuzzy slippers for lounging. I assume since we're staying in a cabin in the woods, there will be a fire. That idea has me giddy. I live in an apartment in the city where, if I'm lucky, our temperatures will drop down into the low sixties. An actual fire, one not of the brush variety that is, sounds amazing.

Can you roast a marshmallow in a fireplace? I don't see why not. It's fire, right?

Lovely, Donna. Your city is showing. I'm a mess.

I double check my packing list and hesitate for only a few seconds before I grab another pair of yoga pants and toss them in my suitcase. Satisfied with my options, I zip it up and slide the beast to the ground. As I place my bags near the door, my phone chimes with an alert that the car I ordered is downstairs. Quickly, I double check that I have my wallet and keys before slipping my carry-on bag onto my shoulder and exiting my apartment.

"Have a good trip, Ms. Moreno." Charlie, the security guard, is more like a bellman with a gun. He's known to hold doors open for all the residents and make small talk, even though none of it is part of his job description. We're lucky to have him and the entire building makes sure to show our appreciation in the form of tips and presents over the holidays.

"Thank you, Charlie. Girl's trip to the snow, if you can believe it."

Eyes wide, he chuckles. "The snow isn't something we see often; you enjoy yourself."

Smiling, I wave my goodbye and exit the building to the waiting car at the curb. Some may see the black sedan as an unnecessary luxury. Truth be told, I have been travelling so much over the last few years that when I sat down with my accountant and looked at my expenses, I was paying for a car I never drove. Add in the car insurance and I'm saving a few hundred a month relying on a car service for trips to and from the airport or using a ride-share.

What I hadn't expected was the cost for a car service when I land in Washington. Of course, the airport I have to fly into for this girl's trip is just shy of one hundred miles from the cabin we're staying in. One hundred miles. In another state. Idaho to be specific. Aggi offered to pick me up, but I didn't want her to have to do all that driving in winter conditions, so I've already decided to bite the bullet and make sure to tip the driver well just for driving in the snow.

My ride to the airport isn't long and I make it through security without an issue. Life as an author means I travel a lot and getting through the security lines has become almost second nature to me. Once

I've slipped into my shoes and fastened my watch, I stop by the chain coffee shop and purchase my traditional splurge on a travel day—a frothy and sugary caramel macchiato with extra whipped cream.

Settling into a seat near my gate, I pull my earbuds from my bag before pulling up my audiobook. Sure it's a little awkward now that I've actually met and talked to Hawk, er, I mean Todd, but as long as I don't have to see him again, I can block the image of him out of my mind while Hawk says all the romantic and sexy words Adeline Snow writes.

"I don't mean to be a pest, but how long do you think it will take us to get to the cabin?" I ask the driver before slipping into the backseat of the small SUV. The bitter cold rips through my body like an open wound. Why do people live where it's this cold?

"About ninety minutes, I'd gather. Of course, as we get to the higher elevation the weather may turn a little, which may add a little time."

The warm leather on my rear is a pleasant surprise. Heated seats. Not something I've had to worry about in the warmer temps of the southwest. Cooling seats, yes. Heated, not so much. I must admit, it's kind of like wrapping up in a heated blanket. I like it.

As we drive, I watch the city quickly fade from something you'd see all across the country to smaller communities just off the side of the interstate. A body of water is just off in the distance. It's strange to me to be driving on a major interstate and there is just water off to the side.

Over the next hour or so, I relax into the seat and take in the view before me. The vast terrain changes from quiet and serene backdrops to small housing communities. The usual grocery chains and fast food restaurant billboards advertise along the highway, and I'll admit they bring a little comfort to this city girl. I'm not going to be that far away from civilization should I need some bright lights. Checking my phone, I don't see any messages from Aggi. She did tell me cell and Wi-Fi service may be spotty at the cabin, so I'm not surprised by her silence.

The last part of our drive is a far cry from the beginning. Long gone are the signs of cities and in its place, a scene comparable to a postcard. Miles and miles of open space lie before me with snowcapped mountains in the distance. The driver slows as we approach a short bridge. A large lake with little patches of ice floating are on either side of us as we approach a sweet small town. My heart rate picks up as I take in the surroundings.

Aggi was right. This is perfect.

The sun is only beginning to set, and as I look at my watch, I note that it sets rather early here. That's funny to me because I remember having a conversation with Aggi once on a late summer night. I was already dressed for bed and settled on top of my fifteen hundred thread count sheets and she was telling me it was barely dusk at her house. How strange that in the winter, our days seem to catch one another but in the summer, her days are much longer. .

"We aren't much further, miss."

"Thank you. This town is lovely. It's almost like a scene out of a movie." I don't add that it is like a scene out of one of my favorite holiday romances.

"We're quite lucky in this part of the country. Our little piece of heaven is growing, which will get you varying opinions on whether or not that's a good thing. I only hope with the growth, we don't lose the small-town feeling like you're seeing now."

I couldn't agree more.

At almost exactly ninety minutes from when I slid into the backseat of the car, we turn down a dark road. Only the moonlight guides us as the driver maneuvers the SUV up a road blanketed by nothing but trees.

"Wow, the cabin must be pretty deep in these woods."

Laughing, he says, "Oh these aren't woods. The home you're headed to actually overlooks the lake. This is just your run-of-the-mill road."

Well, I feel foolish. Scratch that. I felt a little embarrassed at my assumption we were in the woods. I feel *foolish* when I see the home in front of us. Cabin my ass. If this is a cabin, the Mona Lisa is a sketch. There are no logs stacked up to make a wall or a creaky looking wrap around porch. No, before me is something I would call a chalet or mini mansion, but never a cabin.

I don't say anything else as the SUV comes to a stop just before the front door. Quickly, my door opens, and a hand is extended to help me exit the vehicle. Snagging my bag, I allow the man to help me out of the car. Now that I've gawked at the building in front of me, I notice the ground isn't covered in ice or snow. Sure, the surrounding areas are blanketed in the fluffy white stuff but the ground, where I stand, is just wet.

"Do you think the ground is heated like the seats?" I try to joke with the driver and instantly regret it. Surely they don't heat the ground here.

"Yep. A lot of the homes around the lake have heated driveways. The ice buildup makes it pretty slick."

Huh. Heated seats and heated driveways. Who knew?

I take a tentative step toward the front steps, just in case the wet and not icy ground is not as it seems. When I determine it's safe to walk, I make my way to the front steps as my bag is placed next to me.

"Thank you so much for your help and getting me here safely. You weren't kidding when you said the weather may affect the roads."

"You're very welcome. Enjoy yourself." He tips his hat at me and leaves me alone on the porch.

Quickly, the warmth from the heated seats has worn off and a shiver runs down my spine. Thank goodness for my new knee-high boots with fuzzy tops. My tootsies are staying toasty warm, even though the air feels icy on my exposed skin. Even my jeans can't keep the intense cold off my legs.

Looking around, I don't see a doorbell, so I reach for the handle and push on the door. Slowly, I peek my head inside and call Aggi's name. Nothing.

"Hello?" I say a little louder as I pull my luggage into the foyer.

In the distance, I hear the telltale voice of one Justin Timberlake and shake my head at Aggi's choice of music. I had no idea she was a JT fan. I fully support this new information and make my way into the cabin. No, chalet. I refuse to call this amazing place a cabin.

With an open concept, one wall of the room is a rock fireplace complete with a roaring fire inside and a large television hanging above it. Huge plush couches fill the space and I want to throw myself on them and turn on a cheesy romantic comedy while I devour a bowl of popcorn. Turning around, I see a large gourmet style kitchen with top-of-the-line appliances.

But, it isn't the huge refrigerator or the inviting couches that take my breath away, it's the large wall of windows. Stepping up, I take in the beauty before me. Miles and miles of snow-covered trees surround a massive body of water. I assume this is the lake the driver mentioned. If I didn't know I'd freeze my ass off outside, I'd open one of these double doors and step out to take in the beauty. It's so peaceful and serene, I'm not sure I'll ever want to leave. If I can't write a sweet romance here, where can I?

"Hey there."

Screaming I jump around, landing in a karate stance as I take in the man before me. It takes a few seconds for my brain to acknowledge who is standing only steps away. The leprechauns on his shirt should have been my first clue. Todd.

"Holy shit, woman. You scared me."

"I . . . scared . . . *you*?" I rasp out. "You can't sneak up on someone like that. Holy crap, my heart is going to explode." I bend over, trying to catch my breath following my sudden athletic moves and near-death experience, and slow my racing heartbeat.

"Whoa, whoa there. Stand up and put your hands on your head." Lifting my head, I look at Todd but all I see are stars. This is not good. Before I can react, Todd grabs me by the arms and stands me up, placing my hands on my head. He's standing very close to me, his dark eyes wide as he takes in a deep breath and exhales. I begin to mimic him and in only a few attempts, I feel my heart slowing and my breathing regulating.

"You okay?" he asks with a seriousness I haven't seen from him before.

"I think so," I reply, pulling my hands from atop my head. "Wow. Thanks for that. I'm pretty sure I was going down for the count."

"Yeah, you didn't look good. Your color is back now. Why don't you sit down, and I'll get you some water?"

Nodding, I take a seat on the couch, and it's as comfortable and soft as I thought it would be. Todd comes back with a glass of water and full wine glass. Smiling, I accept the water and take a large drink before swapping it out for the wine. When in doubt, wine is the answer.

"Thanks."

"No problemo."

Setting the water on the table, I ask, "Where's Aggi?"

"She didn't tell you?"

"Tell me what?"

Making himself comfortable on the couch across from me, Todd sits back, his arm slung across the cushion. "She's in L.A." Choking on my wine, I wipe the dribbles from my chin and look back at him. "Spencer ate shit or something and has to have surgery. She went there, and I came here."

"Oh no. Is Spencer going to be okay?"

"Yeah, she sent me a text that they are holding off on surgery to further assess the damage. Really all it means is now he's hot *and* injured, which makes him even more of an attraction to the ladies, so Aggi was right to go be with him. But, since she's there with him she asked me to come here and open up the cabin for you."

I snort at his use of the word "cabin" which he completely misinterprets as frustration with her absence. "Don't be mad at her. I'm sure if your fiancé was injured, you'd do the same thing."

"Oh, absolutely. I was snorting at you calling this place a cabin. This is like a small mansion or a chalet, it is not a cabin."

"Eh, potato potahtoe."

Smacking his hands together, I startle and almost spill my wine.

"Now that you're here and all settled, I'm going

to boogie. The sheets are all changed, the fridge is stocked with the long list of essentials Aggi sent me. You should be good on fire wood too. My number is on the fridge if you need anything. I'll see ya."

Wait, what? He's leaving me here? Alone?

"Uh, you're leaving?"

Standing, he furrows his brow at my question. I watch as his look changes from one of confusion to one of flirtation. Waggling his brows, he asks in his Hawk Weaver voice, "You want me stay?"

"Put that"—I begin waving my hand in his direction—"away. This is a girl's weekend. No flirting allowed. So you can go. I'll be fine."

How hard can it be to keep a fire going and relax? I'm a strong independent woman who is going to write a sweet small-town romance and take the indie world by storm. Or at least write about a storm.

Todd laughs and picks up his keys from the counter before turning to me. "You'll be fine. Like I said, gimme a call if you need anything. See ya."

And before I can respond, he walks through the door and into the night.

Chapter 10

Todd

Grabbing my coat, I race out the door, grateful that I paid extra for the heated walkway. Todd and ice don't like each other. And Nurse Chilson has already paid for one child's college education courtesy of moi. She's on her own for the next one.

I could slow my steps but that would keep me in proximity to Donna for longer, and I don't need that. It's not that I have a problem with her. Quite the contrary. After talking with her in Portland, and especially after her asking Hawk Weaver to come out to play, I'm not too proud to admit I did a little internet stalking.

She's fucking amazing. Not only does she remind me of one of those contestants on *America's Top Model*, she's an incredibly savvy business woman. Her marketing plan is solid, focusing on her books' sex appeal and the fantasies of strong, independent women who take what they want with no regrets. Her author ranking and each of her books prove she's doing everything right.

By the description of each story, I suspect many of her female characters are a lot like her on the surface. Beautiful, self-assured, and full of passion and drive.

Donna, on the other hand, is much more. In the limited amount of time we've spent together, I could tell there's more to her than meets the eye. While she's everything she puts into her story, deep down I think there's a version of her begging to come out. She just needs a place to figure that out. Right here in my "chalet" as she called it is probably a good place to start.

And for her to do the soul searching she needs, she doesn't need the distraction of one super sexy narrator—slash—businessman.

Slamming my car door, I shove the key in the ignition of my 2002 Honda Accord and crank the engine. Except . . .

Nothing happens.

Shit, I think as I try again with the clicking sound practically mocking me and the fact that I'm not going anywhere any time soon. What the hell could have killed my battery?

Looking around to try and dispel the mystery, I realize I never turned the light off when I dropped my phone under the seat and went looking for it earlier. That'll do it. Not the smartest move on my part and not at all conducive for leaving Donna to do some soul searching.

Oh well. Looks like her girls' weekend has turned into a dual gender evening.

Climbing out of my car, I ponder how to get back

inside. Do I knock? Just walk in? Will I startle her? Surely she'll realize I'm not gone yet since it's less than two minutes since I walked out.

Decision made, I turn the handle and walk through the door to find my man JT still crooning away and Donna—

Shimmying.

"Having fun?"

"Ahh!" she yells as she spins around and lands in a fighting position again.

"Slow down there, Karate Kid. Last time you did that, you almost passed out."

Fortunately for the both of us, and the corner of the end table which doesn't like having people fall on it, she recognizes me faster this time and continues to breathe.

Straightening, her cheeks tinge with pink from either embarrassment or exertion. It's really anyone's guess.

"You really need to stop sneaking up on me."

"I left only seconds ago. Who else could it have been?"

"Well let's see." Her arms cross over her chest. Uh oh. The lawyer is coming out. I'm in for a verbal sparring session. "I'm in the middle of nowhere in a cabin alone and it's dark out. So Freddy, Jason, or pretty much any cast member of the Scream movies."

"Touché."

Dropping back on the couch, I'm glad to see her

look relaxed already. This trip is already good for her.

"But seriously," she continues, dropping down beside me, "I thought you had to race out of here."

"I thought I did too, but it appears the shagging wagon has different ideas."

She cocks her head at me, one brow practically touching her hairline. "Shagging wagon?"

"Land yacht?" She continues to look at me funny. "Pimp mobile? Four-banger?" Still staring. "My car, Donna."

"Oh I know what all those words mean. I just haven't heard them used in a non-story related way since, oh, the eighties."

It's my turn to look at her funny. At least it makes her laugh.

"Sorry." She covers her mouth with her finger tips. "I'm not trying to be insulting. You're just kind of odd."

Leaning back, I stretch my legs out and lay my head on the cushion. "Odd is in the mind of the beholder."

"That's not how the saying goes."

"I'm the beholder, so in my mind it does."

This time she laughs out loud. I can't contain my smirk. I like the sound of her happiness.

"Okay, okay. I concede. But really, why are you back? I don't mind. Just curious."

Sighing, I'm finally ready to admit my failure. "I left the dome light on in my car."

"Oh, that sucks. Is someone coming to give you a jump?"

This is the part where her city girl knowledge is completely useless. Maybe it's a good thing I'm not leaving her alone on her first night. I bet she doesn't even know how to keep a fire going.

"Holy shit," I exclaim. "Do you know how to keep a fire going?"

"Yes." She looks around, refusing to make eye contact with me. "Maybe."

Narrowing my eyes at her, I can't help but press the issue. "How." I don't even ask. I basically demand proof that she won't die of hypothermia if the power were to go out.

"You . . ." she lifts her hands up, hands clenched like she's holding something and starts jabbing at the air. "Stoke it."

Turning to face her, I cross my arms. "And?"

"And . . . blow on it, I don't know, okay?" Her admission of defeat makes me laugh. "I have no idea how to keep a fire going so you should probably cancel that jump for your car so I don't accidentally live in the forest wrong."

Once I finally stop laughing, I let her in on a little secret. "Donna, no one is coming up here to jump my car."

"What?"

"Honey, it's dark out. No one is gonna brave these roads with a storm getting ready to blow in."

Her head whips around to look out the window. Sadly, the only thing she's going to see now is our reflection because of the dark. "There's a storm coming?"

"Not a big one. Just enough to keep people at home for the night," I say with a shrug. "It's pretty normal around here. And Old Man Davies is the only mechanic in town who would be willing to come out and help, but since it's after hours, I'm positive he's already at least one and a half sheets to the wind."

That eyebrow of hers goes up again. "Let me guess, not quite drunk yet but enough that you won't want him anywhere near the driver's side of a car?"

I tap my nose. "You got it."

She takes a deep breath and nods. "Yeah, it's really different here, and I've only been glamping for an hour so far."

"Welcome to small-town life. Now," I say, patting her leg and standing up to face her, "are you an unpacker or a live out of the suitcase kind of girl?"

She huffs with humor. "I'm on a working vacation. Of course I'm living out of the suitcase."

"Well, then go roll your monstrosity of a suitcase into the master bedroom—"

"Hey, it's full of winter clothes!"

"—so you can change, and I'm going to go make us a hearty meal."

"You can cook?"

Pointing at myself, I let her in on another puzzle

piece that is the life of Todd. "Born and raised by a single mom who refused to wait on me hand and foot. I can make a mean cheese and cracker plate."

"That actually sounds perfect."

"Good. Now hop to it, lady. We've got to get a move on. Blake Shelton won't watch himself."

She pauses, mid-rise. "Blake Shelton?"

I stare at her, mouth half open in shock. "Please don't tell me you've never watched *The Voice*. I don't want to have to kick you out into the snow tonight."

"Don't worry about me. I'll just hang out on the fancy heated driveway."

"Good call. With a couple of blankets, you could probably survive the night."

"Fortunately"—she completes her rise and puts her hands on her hips—"I *have* seen *The Voice* before, so any blankets in this house are staying on the beds tonight."

I wipe my brow in mock relief. "Don't do that to me. I think my heart missed a few beats."

She has the wherewithal to roll her eyes at me. Just for that, I might keep the smoked gouda for myself.

"I think your heart will be fine," she says condescendingly as she walks by patting my arm. "Now go make me some food."

"On it." I mock salute. "Master bedroom is at the very end of the hall."

I turn toward the kitchen but stop when the reflection of Donna walking away distracts me from my steps. Damn. She's beautiful, smart, and witty as a clam. Too bad it's Hawk Weaver she wants, not Todd Chimolski.

Chapter 11

Donna

I lied. I've never watched The Voice. I'm sure it's a good show but reality competition shows have never been my thing. While I love music, I love the written word more.

Still, the look on Todd's face had me concerned he was going to have a myocardial infarction on the spot, so I fibbed a little. Plus, I'm probably the only person in America who hasn't seen the show. I didn't want to seem weird.

Not that the guy who sports ugly shirts and recites incorrect phrases would judge me. Or maybe he would. He seems to have an unnatural crush on Blake Shelton. That surprises me a little after hearing his music choice when I walked in the door. Which is exactly what led me to open my secret playlist and shake my ass to my own JT favorite song before he busted me.

Doing as instructed, I drag my suitcase down the hall to the master bedroom. The door is ajar, but the room is as dark as the night. Feeling around aimlessly on the wall, I find the light switch and flick it on. The lights on the ceiling fan come to life and I'm blown away by what I see. The room is very similar to the main living space. The colors are in the same palette and the far wall has a beautiful armoire that is twice the size of any piece of furniture I've owned. The massive king size bed is at least five feet off the ground and the plush white bedding and plethora of pillows is begging for me to hop on it and snuggle in for a good night's sleep. *Have no fear pillows, we'll be one very soon.*

Settling my suitcase on the floor against the far wall, I quickly open it and pull out a pair of yoga pants and an oversized T-shirt. Relaxation isn't going to be an issue this weekend, but the first step to that is peeling myself out of these jeans. As I step into the large bathroom, I pause in pure awe. A large tub with a huge window I'm sure has a view to die for, is nestled in the corner. Just past it is a shower that could easily fit four adults and still have room to move around. *A sex shower.* Or at least in one of my books, it would be a sex shower. This tub though, that's all me. I hope there's a bath bomb or at least some bath crystals in one of these drawers.

Letting out a loud rumble, my stomach reminds me I'm starving. Working double time, I change my clothes and pull my hair into a top knot, securing it with a large claw clip. Pausing to take in my appearance, I hear a roar of applause wafting through the house and know Todd has turned on his show.

Padding my way down the hall, I pause in the entryway to the living room where Todd is lounging on the couch. In one hand is a bottle of beer while the other holds a remote control. I look at the large television and see the numbers indicating the volume on the incline. As the numbers rise, so does the voice of the host as he fills the room.

"Do we have to blow an eardrum to listen to this?"

Sputtering his beer, Todd leans forward and coughs before turning his gaze to me. "Yes."

Laughing, I take the spot on the opposite end of the couch where a fresh glass of wine sits next to a very sad attempt at a charcuterie plate. Strewn haphazardly on a large wooden cutting board is a pile of crackers, two blocks of cheese with a knife sticking out of one of them, and a bowl of grapes.

"No Cheese Whiz?" I ask as I pop a grape in my mouth.

"Sadly, no. I was shopping for Aggi and not myself. Are you also a fan of processed cheese?"

"Oh yeah. Fake cheese is the best. I do prefer it on a pile of tortilla chips though."

Nodding in agreement, Todd eyes me over the rim of his bottle as he takes a sip. The look on his face has the hair on the back of my neck standing up. Not in a creepy horror movie killer sort of way but more in a "if he says anything in a Hawk Weaver voice, I won't be responsible for what happens" kind of way.

No. No. What the hell? He wears shirts with leprechauns and listens to reality competition shows at full volume. Not my type at all. Breaking eye contact, I take the knife from the block of cheese and keep myself busy slicing it into cracker size pieces as he turns his attention back to the screen.

We sit in comfortable silence as the competitors belt out not only modern top forty hits but also a few classics as well. I'm not saying I plan to set my DVR to record future episodes, but I will admit I don't exactly mind this. Some of these kids are truly talented.

"What are you doing?" I ask as Todd stands and raises his arms above his head stretching. The jeans lie low on his hips allowing the band of his underwear to peek out from the waistband. Color me surprised. I would've pegged Todd as a tighty whities kind of guy, not boxers. They aren't even boxer briefs. Todd is an old school checkered boxers guy.

"Uh, replenishing our refreshments. We have two more episodes to go."

"Two? How long is this show on for?"

Lowering his arms, Todd turns his attention to me, staring for a few beats, never blinking. Okay, that's creepy. I didn't know we were in a staring contest but here we are. It's only seconds but my eyes are burning, and I need him to blink. *Come on, Todd. Blink.* Nothing. Dammit.

Waving the proverbial white flag, I blink multiple times in quick recession. Tears fill my eyes and my eyeballs jump for joy. I don't think my eyes burned that bad when I was a kid. Or, if they did, I was too busy doing victory laps to care.

"I have three recorded. I rarely watch anything live. I hate the commercials and if I record them, I can watch that much faster. Fast forward is my friend."

"It's recorded? Then why didn't you fast forward through that awful dog caller woman?"

"You seemed to enjoy her rendition of *Proud Mary*, I didn't want to end it too soon for you."

Rolling my eyes, I pick up my empty wine glass in one hand and the tray of snacks in the other before making my way to the kitchen. Quickly, I wrap up the cheese and place it in the refrigerator and also refill my glass with the open bottle of wine in the door. I've made it three steps out of the kitchen when I notice Todd on his knees before the fireplace. He has the large poker in his hand and is moving around the coals.

He may not have the body of a cover model or any of the suits I've been dating lately, but Todd does have a nice ass. Bringing my glass to my lips, I slowly sip as I admire the way he moves on the floor, filling the fireplace with fresh logs. The snap and crackle of the fire is something I've only ever seen on television or imagined in my mind. Flashes of a scene in the book I'm writing pops in my head and I set my glass down on the breakfast bar and rush to my room to grab my laptop.

Pulling it from my carry-on, I open the lid and tap the power button as I walk down the hall back to the living room. Scooping up my glass, I settle back into my spot on the couch and am typing in my passcode when Todd bumps my knee as he resumes his spot on the couch. This time, he's sitting a little closer than he was before.

"If you'd rather watch something else, we can."

Looking at him confused, I don't respond but his

eyes glance to my computer and the realization of what he's saying hits me. "Oh! No, I had a flash of a scene for my book. If I don't get it down, I will likely lose it the minute my head hits the pillow. Although, now that you've offered—"

"Nope. We're watching another episode." Todd reaches for the remote control and brings the show back to life. Although he proclaimed his reasons for recording the show, he doesn't fast forward through the beginning. I assume it's to allow me enough time to do my thing.

I quickly tap out my notes and close my laptop. Settling into the corner of the couch, I bring my feet up and turn to my side, resting my head on the back cushion. The next four contestants are all talented and the judges get into a few heated battles attempting to sway the contestants their way. I think the debates among the coaches may be my favorite part of this show. Well, and the in-depth stories they feature. Cue the tears.

"That right there is one talented youngin'."

Lifting my head, I furrow my brow and ask, "What's with the accent?"

"I need to perfect my southern accent in case I need it for a book. It's why I like Blake so much."

Shaking my head, I chuckle before taking a sip of my wine. It's been a long time since I've just hung out and did nothing but simple conversation, a glass of wine, and mindless television. I'm always chasing a deadline or working on behind the scenes business stuff. I never take time to simply relax. That's something I'll need to change. Maybe not every night but at least once a week.

Turning my attention back to the screen, the young man speaking intrigues me. He's about twenty years old, but his story is one of a man twice his age. Gah, this is the stuff that kills me and at the same time, inspires me. This young man is chasing his dreams. With all the cards stacked against him, he's putting himself out there and trying. He doesn't care if he gets all four chairs to turn for him or none do, he just wants his chance to show the world his talent.

He's a risk taker. The parallels of what he's saying and what I've been thinking of doing with my next book aren't lost on me. I can take a risk. I *need* to take a risk. I'll never know if I don't try.

"He—" I begin to say to Todd when he starts singing along with the contestant. The young man is phenomenal. His voice is strong, and his stage presence is unlike any of the others on this current episode. Todd on the other hand, leaves quite a bit to be desired.

"What are you doing?" I ask, barely controlling the laughter begging to be released.

"Singing."

"No. You're *trying* to sing. But, why?"

Huffing, he picks up the remote and mutes the television just as all four of the judges' chairs spin. "Pause that, I like the battle for the contestant." With a raised brow, Todd smirks and pauses the show before turning his attention back to me.

"Why am I singing?" I nod. "I like to be prepared for anything." Confused, I tilt my head as if doing so will help me understand what he's talking about. "What if I decide to work with another author and it's a rockstar romance? I need to be ready for anything."

This time I don't hold back the laughter. A full belly laugh escapes me. Tears shortly follow, and I have to brace myself from falling off the couch and onto the plush carpeting. "You—" I shout, trying to stop the laughter. After a few seconds, I manage to pull myself together enough to look at Todd. He looks less amused, which only makes me laugh more.

"You do know if you were to do a rockstar book, you wouldn't actually sing, right?"

"It's called method acting."

The laughter picks up again and as I open my mouth to tease him more, the lights flicker.

"Crap."

"Wha—" I begin as the room goes dark. The only light filling the room comes from the roaring fire.

"Power's out. I was afraid of that. They've been doing a little construction down the road."

The power is out? There's no power? That means there's no heat. No running water. My heart begins to race, and I jump from my spot on the couch. Turning to walk, I slam directly into the corner of the table and let out a yelp. Large hands grip my waist and steady me before I fall. Warm breath tickles my ear and I shiver. Not from the cold or from fear but from the way it feels on my skin. Warm. Hot. Sexy.

No. No. No. Not sexy. Not hot. Not . . . well, it is warm but that's neither here nor there.

"Careful there," Todd says. Scratch that, *Hawk Weaver* says.

"I told you to put that away. No Hawk Weaver here." Stepping out of his grip, I turn to face him, crossing my arms over my chest.

"I didn't . . . Oh, I guess I did. Sorry. It slipped. Turns out Hawk is really me when I'm trying to be helpful."

If only he could see me, he'd know I'm rolling my eyes at him.

"It looks like it's going to be an early night for us. I think we should probably get our beds set up and I'll make sure the fire is going good."

"Beds?"

"Yeah, there's no power. We're going to have to sleep out here. Might as well make ourselves comfortable in front of the fire. It'll be like indoor camping."

I watch as Todd begins moving things around and walks toward a large built-in along the wall and pulls a few items from a drawer. I feel kind of stupid standing here doing nothing, I can't see but a foot in front of me, despite the glow from the fire. Todd, however, seems to be part bat and able to see in the dark.

"Are you Batman?" I ask with a snigger.

"What?"

"You can see in the dark. Like a bat."

"Nope. All man."

I'm beginning to agree with that assessment. "How do you know where everything is?" I ask as he turns on a large lantern shaped flashlight. Walking toward me, he smiles and hands me the lantern.

"Because I own it."

"You own this lantern?"

Laughing he shakes his head. "The cabin. It's mine."

My eyes go wide, and I suck in air. "Why do you look surprised?"

"Because your car is broken down on the driveway."

"So?"

"So you have a broken-down car and also the most beautiful house in the woods I've ever seen. That makes no sense."

"Donna." The way he says my name, it's not quite patronizing but it is a little disappointed, maybe? "The car gets me from point A to point B. Real estate is an investment. Ask Dave Ramsey."

He owns this place? The chalet? A man who wears leprechauns and pineapples on his shirts and sings horribly off key as a form of method acting. He owns a home that is probably worth more than my net worth for the last three years combined.

"I'm going need something stronger than wine tonight," I mumble as I take the lantern and walk to the wet bar in the corner and pour myself two fingers of whiskey, taking a tentative sip.

"Don't drink too much. We need to make our bed."

"Our what?"

"No power. We need to make a bed here on the floor and sleep in front of the fire to stay warm. I thought we established this already."

My eyes widen at his words and I toss back the rest of the whiskey. Make a bed. Together? "One bed?" I croak out.

"Body heat is the only way to stay warm. Check the survival guide on the coffee table. But first, chop, chop." He actually claps his hands at me to get moving. "It's going to be a long night."

He can say that again.

Chapter 12

Todd

I wake up to bright light shining in my face. The best part of this place is wall-to-wall windows when you want to see the view.

The worst part of this place is wall-to-wall windows when you want to sleep in the living room.

Plus, the sunshine is making me very hot. And heavy. Like if I rolled over, I'd be rolling on a body.

No . . . wait . . . that's actually a body. Why the hell is there a body in bed with me and why is the person attached to it trying to strangle me?

My hand whips up to my neck to frantically remove the tiny bits of thread that are being used to cut off my air supply sending me to a slow and painful death. Am I the male version of the woman with the green ribbon around her neck now? Will my head fall off if I yank too hard? . . . wait. Nope. That's not thread. That's hair.

Donna's hair, to be exact. It's soft and silky and smells like hydrangeas and that thought is way too serial killer creepy even for me. I quickly toss her hair back over to her side of the pallet we made on the floor, more awake now that I've had to fight to stay alive.

I knew telling ghost stories last night was a bad idea. It's not the nightmares that get me. It's those few seconds the next morning when I'm not quite awake that always freak me out.

Donna begins to stir, probably from the hair that just landed on her face, so I freeze, not sure how all of this is going to play out. A million possibilities ranging from her accusing me of trying to accost her to her realizing her undying love and devotion for me. I need to be prepared for anything. The arm draped across my mid-section jerks, and I suck in a breath, waiting for her next move.

I watch as she pushes up on her elbows and moves those killer hairs off her face. She looks disheveled and confused. Beautiful. She's breathtaking in the morning light.

Seriously. I have to stop reading Aggi's books if I want to keep my balls.

Taking a deep breath and sighing it out, Donna looks over at me, her eyes narrowed with sleep and her brow furrowed. "What happened?"

"Power went out. We made a pallet on the floor."

"I know that part. How did you end up on my side?"

Looking down at the make-shift bed, I scoff. "I am clearly on my side of the bed. Which means you ended up next to me."

She rolls her eyes. "I highly doubt that." Ouch. "I don't usually move when I sleep." Less ouch.

"Well, you don't usually sleep next to me. It's okay though. I understand," I continue, trying to lighten the awkward mood. "I probably started talking in my sleep. I'd snuggle up next to Hawk Weaver under those circumstances too."

Donna drops her face into her pillow, shoulders shaking as she laughs. When she finally comes up for air, she pushes off the cushions to stand up. No sooner does she rise from the floor, than the room fills with a shrieking teenage mother and small child through the speakers of the television. She startles, looks from me to the television before she says, "Okay, on that note, I'm going to spend my first official day of vacation taking a much-needed bubble bath."

I reach for the remote control on the table and flip off the television. "You've scoped out the tub in the master, I see."

"I've been dreaming about it all night."

She's been dreaming about the tub but snuggling next to Hawk Weaver? Hawk should be offended. But he's not and neither am I.

"There are a couple of bath explosions or whatever under the sink, and I think you'll find the towels to your liking."

She stops and cocks one eyebrow at me. "Explosions? You mean bath bombs?" I shrug and nod, explosions or bombs. Whatever they are, they look like Easter threw up in the form of balls. "Please tell me they're the biggest, fluffiest towels you could find."

"Even bigger and fluffier. I had them imported

from a famous spa in the Swiss Alps."

"Really?" Her eyes are wide as saucers.

"No."

She shakes her head and turns to walk away. "I'll be sure to let management know if they're not up to my standards, then."

I chuckle at her quip and lie back, dropping my arm over my eyes to block out the sun while my body continues waking up. If I had been told a week ago I was going to spend the night with Donna Moreno snuggled up against me, I would have completely agreed out loud, while thinking that was a crazy notion in my head.

Yet here I am, with intimate knowledge of what a hot mess she is first thing in the morning. The best part—she's not the slightest bit embarrassed about it. She never freaked out about morning breath or raccoon eyes or the rat's nest on her head. She just rolled over and started bantering with me.

I like that kind of confidence in a woman. Too bad she didn't realize it was me she was curled up against until it was over.

Oh well. No time to wallow, I think as I push myself up to the standing position. It's . . . fuck, seven in the morning?

I groan and rub my hand down my face. Stupid wall of windows. I could have slept for another two hours. Instead, I make my way to one of the other two bathrooms in the house and break open a new toothbrush before climbing into the shower. Although I don't live here full-time, I do spend some time in this place, so I keep a few items stored in the owner's locked closet for times like this.

Once I've slipped on my favorite Christmas balls shirt, I take a moment to admire the greatness. Balls. It's a shirt covered in balls and my favorite for the obvious reason of the male genitalia jokes I get to tell at the expense of other people's discomfort. I head back out to the living room for a quick check of my voice mail then begin cleaning up.

Two of the blankets are folded and all four pillows are stripped, because nothing says slumber party better than a soft place to lay your head, when my phone alerts Aggi is calling me.

I freeze like a deer caught in the headlights. She can't know I'm here. There is literally nothing happening, but I feel like last night was something Donna and I want to keep to ourselves. Not because it's a secret but because . . . well, I don't know. I also don't know why I'm standing like a stone statue, Aggi can't see me through the phone. Yet, here I stand, like an idiot, in the living room.

Rolling my eyes at my own reaction I grab the phone and swipe before it goes to voicemail. "Yelllo."

"How did it go."

"What? No hello, Todd? No how are you doing, Todd?"

"Hello, Todd. How are you doing, Todd," she deadpans. Doesn't even bother with inflection. It appears that every woman in my life is trying to push my buttons these days. Joke's on them, I'm not easily pushed, well at least my buttons aren't.

"I'm great, thanks. How's Spencer? Getting sympathy from all the ladies, I'm sure."

She lets out a snort laugh. "He would be if he wasn't such a big baby. If this is what having a toddler is like, I'm not sure I ever want kids." I shudder at the thought of either of us having kids. We're the most irresponsible people I know. Sometimes I wonder how we've survived this long, and lord knows it's a miracle our mothers kept us alive to adulthood. "The doctor is still undecided about surgery. Wants to wait another week to do an additional scan and see how it's healing."

"Lucky bastard."

"For being injured?"

"No for having surgery. You know hospital pudding is my favorite."

"I'll be sure to swipe you some and bring it back with me."

Picking up the last blanket off the floor, I toss it over the back of the couch. "Which won't be for a while, will it?"

She sighs a heavy sigh. "No. Probably not. I was trying to crank out this book so I could get here for some R&R but it looks like I'm going to have to work in L.A. for a while."

"You say that like it's a bad thing."

"It just messes with my flow, is all. You know I like to get out and write in public. It seems to keep me on track better. But if I'm playing nursemaid I can't exactly go anywhere."

"Just hop him up on those painkillers when you need to leave. He'll never know you're gone."

"I'll keep that in mind. Anyway . . ."

My guard immediately goes up. She's about to ask me about Donna, I just know it. I have to be very careful how I answer. Aggi has always been able to sense panic in my voice.

"Were you able to let Donna in the cabin? She's not mad, is she?"

Focus, Todd. Stay calm.

"Everything is good to go. I got some supplies and settled her in. So she's settled in. All settled. Yep. Settled. In."

"Todd . . ."

I grimace. Here we go.

"Why do you sound nervous?"

Think faster, Todd!

"I'm ad libbing. Practicing for sounding hysterical and manly at the same time in case you ever decide to write a murder mystery."

Eh. Not my best work, but it'll have to do.

"That's . . . weird. But not terribly surprising coming from you. Speaking of narrating, though, I've been listening to the sample you sent over of the next book. Why do I hear sneezing in the background?"

Sneezing?

"Fucking Bill. I told him he needed antibiotics for that sinus infection." And thank you Bill for giving me a topic change I can work with.

Aggi laughs brightly, clearly already forgetting the nerves in my voice. Now if only Donna will stay in the bath for a little longer . . . and I have to stop thinking about Donna in the bath. I can't play that off. Hawk Weaver is very, very bad at keeping the sexy out of his voice.

"Poor Bill," Aggi says sympathetically. "He's been dealt a rough hand."

"Yeah well, that hand better stay on the other side of his apartment when I start narrating the final version," I mutter, making a mental note to have a little chat with my building manager. And the construction foreman. Maybe they can do something about the noise between levels. It'll need to be addressed before resale anyway.

Aggi babbles on for a little longer about the warmth of L.A. and her latest book. It doesn't take long, though, to hear Spencer complaining in the background. She's right; he does sound like a toddler.

"I gotta go, Todd," she says hurriedly. "If I don't get these pain meds in him soon, it's going to get drastically more annoying in the next ten minutes."

"At least you'll be able to write sometime in the next half hour once he passes out."

"Or I'll be fighting off him being handsy. The meds seem to make him horny."

"Ah!" I yell and throw my finger into the ear not attached to my phone. "I don't need to know this shit!

You know what? I think the connection is getting bad. *Wheeeeeee* . . ." I do my best impression of wind in a tunnel. "Yep. Hear that? Definitely a bad connection."

"Todd—"

"Nope. *Wheeeeeeee* . . ."

"Todd!"

"Gotta go before we lose service. *Wheeeee* . . ." Quickly I hang up the phone and throw it onto the couch, as if getting it far from me will scrub the visual images of horny Spencer out of my mind.

"Was that Aggi on the phone?"

I look up and Donna momentarily stuns me. Her hair is in a braid over one shoulder and she's wearing jeans and an oversized cable knit sweater, which is shrugged down over one shoulder. With the early morning lighting, she looks angelic.

That's another point in favor of the giant wall of windows and another point against reading romance books.

Shaking off my daze, I let out a long exhale. Apparently, I was holding a breath. Huh. That's new.

"Uh, yeah. She was just checking on you. Making sure I didn't forget to let you in or something and you ended up spending the night on the porch."

She smiles, and I'm taken aback again. What is going on here? Do these windows have magical powers?

"Did you tell her you spent the night?"

Magic is over. Clearly Donna has lost her mind. "Hell no. If she knew I was still here because I forgot to turn the light off in my car, I'd never hear the end of it."

Donna smiles and drops down on the couch, her legs bent underneath her. "I'm sorry you're still stuck. If I had a car, I'd drive you to work."

Finishing folding the blankets, I wave her off. "Oh I'm not stuck. Old Man Davies left me a message before we woke up. He was here three hours ago."

"Wait." She glances at the clock. "He jumped your car at five in the morning?"

I shrug. "He's old. Has been getting up that early since I've known him. Probably why he has dinner at four in the afternoon."

"Huh. Um, I don't mean to be rude, but if your car is working why are you still here?"

"It's my house."

She rolls her eyes playfully. "I know that. Don't you have a job to get to?"

I shrug nonchalantly again. "The boss won't care. Besides, I haven't had breakfast yet."

"So?"

"So you're trying to write a sweet romance, right?"

"Yesss . . ."

"You've got a whole town full of sweet romance inspiration right at your fingertips. Let's get some breakfast and see where your ideas take you."

The slow grin that crosses her face is a new look for me. Suddenly, doing Aggi's dirty work doesn't seem like such a hardship after all.

Chapter 13

Donna

When Todd suggested we go into town to explore and allow me to find inspiration, I was equally excited and nervous. Excited because I want to be inspired. I want, no need, to get outside of my head and my normal creative process if I'm going to really put my best foot forward with this sweet romance. The nerves were a product of him. More specifically, his sometimes lack of filter, random Christmas shirt, and perhaps not so accidental slip of his Hawk Weaver voice.

Excitement overshadowed the nervousness, though, and I quickly retreated to my room to grab gloves, a scarf, my winter coat, and snow boots. I bought these babies specifically for this trip. The fashionista in me is excited to finally show them off.

And now I'm overheating like someone put a heating pad under my ass. Todd, on the other hand, is sitting comfortably in his Christmas balls shirt and jeans. He doesn't even have on snow boots, just some hiking looking boots.

We sit in comfortable silence as we drive down the mountain, and I'm grateful I couldn't see much last night. The road isn't dangerous per se but if I allow myself the opportunity, my overactive imagination will have us plummeting to our death. I don't need that thought in my head. Ever.

Instead, I look at the beautiful snow-capped trees. Pulling my cell phone from my purse, I snap a few pictures that should help me with descriptions later in my story.

Fanning myself with my hand, I let out a breath, the coolness a brief blessing to the heat my skin is projecting.

"You should dump that jacket. It isn't too cold out and most places will have the heat on. You'll just end up carrying it the entire time."

Looking from the outside where everything is covered in snow to Todd and back again, I say, "It's freezing out. How can you suggest it's not cold?"

Shrugging he responds, "It's cold enough to snow but really after a few minutes I doubt you'll notice it. Your sweater is pretty thick, and you have on your boots, so your feet won't get wet."

As he turns into a parking space in front of a small café, I contemplate his suggestion. And immediately dismiss it. He can't possibly think I won't freeze. The temperature drops to eighty at home and I put on a sweater.

I open my door and meet Todd on the sidewalk. The cold air is a welcome greeting as it helps regulate me from the internal temperature I had in the car. I briefly wonder if that's a small snippet of what menopause is going to be like someday. That's going to suck.

"How about a little grub before we explore? This place has the absolute best biscuits and gravy."

"Sounds great. I'm starving." I am starving but, in my head, begin calculating how much exercise I'll have to do, or how much wine and cheese I'll have to sacrifice, if I were to indulge in the biscuits and gravy. Too much but damn it sounds good

Todd opens the door to the café and a bell chimes as I step into the inviting space. Booths line the far wall with tables for two filling the rest of the space. This place can't possibly seat more than forty people but it's absolutely perfect. My senses are in overload as I inhale the aromas of maple syrup, bacon, and coffee. Agreeing with the great smells filling the space, my stomach grumbles its appreciation.

"Was that you?" Todd asks.

"Just get us a table," I retort. My tone is teasing but I'm also slightly embarrassed.

"Let's take that table by the window. That way you can people watch and really start your recon."

"Recon?" I bark out in a laugh as I walk toward the table he suggested.

Stripping off the heater also known as my coat, I hang it off the back of my chair and sit down, flipping the coffee cup sitting on the table over to indicate my desire and absolute need for caffeine. The décor of the café is simple and homey; deep burgundies and floral patterns adorn each table cloth while a single bud vase sits nestled between the salt and pepper and sweetener.

"Yeah, recon for your book. You'll get a good vantage point of the people walking up and down the streets. You'll also see most aren't wearing a big down coat either."

"Are you going to tease me about my coat the entire day?" I ask, crossing my arms over my chest.

"Nah," he says mimicking my stance only raising a brow instead of pursing his lips. I try, and fail, to keep a stern look in response. "Just a couple more hours."

"Good morning. Coffee?" the waitress asks as she pours our coffee.

"Morning, Lisa. How's it going?"

"Well Todd, it's going about the same as it was yesterday when you came in. My kid is still a little shit, my husband was up early plowing, and you're still not willing to date my cousin."

The sarcasm dripping from the waitress makes me giggle. I love that Todd takes her jabs in stride even if he likely deserves them. Smirking as they continue bantering, I pour a little creamer into my cup and stir it when I feel Todd kick me under the table. Glancing up at him, I shrug and smile as he chuckles and shakes his head. I'm busted.

"But, considering this is your date today, I can't say I blame you for not wanting to take Cindy out. Hi, I'm Lisa. I don't think we've met." I look at the hand extended to me and up at the woman introducing herself.

"Donna Moreno," I say, shaking her hand. "Your place is fantastic."

"Thanks, we like it. It's been in my family for three generations. What brings you to town, Donna?"

Wow, she just gets right to it. No boundaries here.

"Oh, I'm staying at—"

"She's friends with Aggi," Todd says, cutting me off. Well, that was rude. "She'll be staying at the cabin for a few days, but I wanted to show her around a bit. Give this city girl a little small-town experience."

"That's nice of you. If you needed a little small-town experience, you've come to the right spot. Of course, we have an influx of tourism right now with the recent storms. I heard the mountain got at least nine inches last night."

"Nine inches you say?" Todd purrs in his Hawk Weaver voice.

Lisa and I look at each, exchanging dramatic eye rolls.

"And on that note, are you ready to order or need a minute?"

"I need more than a minute," Todd mumbles to himself. I'm sure he's trying to get a laugh out of us, but Lisa and I both ignore him.

I haven't even opened the menu on the table to see what my options are, but before I can ask for more time, Todd orders for both of us. As Lisa walks away, he turns his attention to me and picks up his coffee cup. "What?" he asks when he notices the stunned expression on my face. "You're on vacation and embracing small-town life. Let the food happen, Donna. Let it happen."

My instinct is to argue. To tell him he shouldn't have ordered for me. I shouldn't indulge in the bacon, side of hash browns, and sausage gravy and biscuits he ordered. But I don't. I don't because dammit I'm starving, and it all sounds amazing.

"I'm not agreeing but," I say with a dramatic sigh, "I'm conceding. Like pleading no contest or something."

"Oh sweet, Donna. Whatever helps you sleep at night. Speaking of, we need get some marshmallows for the fire. I saw the way you were ogling those flames. I bet you've never indulged in a little creamy goodness in your mouth."

Sputtering my coffee, I begin to choke. In only a few gasps for air, I see stars. Todd jumps from his seat and is slapping his open palm on my back in seconds. His reaction turns my choking to laughter.

"Are you okay? I didn't even think of what I was saying, the words just happened. We should blame Aggi and her damn books. I say the word 'dick' and 'climax' so much when I'm working, the innuendos are like second nature."

"Todd, sit down and stop trying to kill the poor woman. Two short stacks, a large side of hash browns, and half a pig." Lisa's voice leaves no room for argument. She sets the plates, which are more like platters, of food on our table before promising to return with more coffee.

Eyeing me across the table, Todd tilts his head from side to side as I wipe the tears from my cheeks. It isn't lost on me that with Todd around, his humor and laid-back attitude surrounding us both, I'm at ease. I've laughed, teased, and picked at him like he's an old friend more than I have with anyone else in years. Relaxed and ready to see what he has in store for us, I stab my fork into a large sausage link and bring it to my mouth.

As my teeth sink into the deliciousness, I release a moan. I'm not sure if it's the mountain air, the fact that I'm completely relaxed, or the man who is staring at me, mouth agape, but this is the best damn sausage of my life.

Two hours, a discarded coat, and a side cramp from laughing later, Todd and I are approaching the last store on First Avenue and our final stop of this "Donna gets to know small town USA" tour. Yes, last. Meaning, there have been multiple. As in all.

I thought at first, he would take me to a few shops, maybe grab a coffee somewhere while he told me stories of the town and its people. Show me a little inspiration so I can head back to the cabin and get some work done. He didn't. Instead, he played tour guide extraordinaire and took me from store to store, introducing me to the people who make up this sleepy little town.

Everyone has been kind and welcoming, answering the random and rather strange questions Todd asked each of them. "Would you rather be a cougar or a moose?" "Do you think lights in the city are brighter than the moon?" "Do you say pop or soda?"

Nobody batted an eye. They accepted his randomness with the most gracious, if not confused, response. But it was the young woman in the small market who was clearly his biggest fan. Marcy offered him the brightest of smiles but the blush that dusted her cheeks when he asked her questions about the store and her position, told me she might have a little crush on my new friend. I watched as she lit up and spoke of the small business with gratitude and the owners with the utmost respect.

Watching Todd with her, the kindness and interest he exuded, I found myself wanting to know him more. Beyond his jokes and weird clothing choices, lies a man with a huge heart and love of people.

Like most of the shops on this street, a bell signals our arrival. Todd holds the door open, motioning for me to enter but instead, I pause and look up at him, my hand resting on his forearm.

"Thank you."

"For?" he asks, brows furrowed.

"Thank you for taking the time with me today. I'm sure there were a million other places you could have been or things you'd rather be doing. I appreciate you showing me around and helping me understand small-town life."

I do believe I've embarrassed him. A light blush appears on the apples of his cheeks and knowing he doesn't realize how great he's been makes me smile. Not saying another word, I step into *Christmas 365* and am blown away.

Cheerful holiday music wafts from the speakers and the scent of cinnamon and pine fill the air. Trees of varying shapes and sizes are adorned in ornaments ranging from hand-painted balls to traditional snowmen and Santa hats. Nostalgia hits me in the face and I'm transported to simpler times. Times when life didn't force me to run at a thousand miles an hour, survive on little to no sleep, and push myself to the point of exhaustion that I have nothing left to give but snark and tears.

"It's pretty spectacular, isn't it?"

Looking at him over my shoulder, I smile. "It's magical." Turning in a circle to take it all in, I furrow my brow. "But it's February. People still shop here after the holidays?"

"This is a big tourist town. Not sure the store sells a lot of decorations before October, but tourists always want ornaments of the places they've traveled."

Makes perfect sense to me. I wouldn't mind finding one myself.

Glancing to my right, I see a mid-size tree that is decorated in a more modern style. Ornaments that are more on the kitschy side draw my attention and I approach the tree. Sitting alone on a branch is a typewriter. Bright turquoise with old fashioned keys, it's adorable. Plucking it from the tree, Todd takes the piece of perfection and walks toward the counter where an older woman sits with a weathered paperback in her hands

Ignoring what he's doing, and the sadness in my heart over him swooping in and taking the ornament, I peruse a little more while he makes his purchase. A few minutes later, as I'm bent over looking at a classic Santa's village, I hear "Ready to blow this pop stand?" and jump straight up, knocking into a display with my flailing arms.

"Didn't we talk about you sneaking up on me?"

"Hey, let's be grateful you weren't trying to karate chop my head again. I'd call this progress. So, you ready to head back to the cabin? Have enough inspiration for the day?"

Steadying my heartbeat, I take a deep breath and nod. Walking ahead of me, Todd opens the door and again waves me forward. As soon as we step out onto the street, I begin walking toward where the car is parked when he reaches for my hand, stopping me in my tracks. Warmth runs from my hand up my arm, but the action has the opposite effect on me and I shiver as I turn to face him.

"A little something to remember your time here," he says, holding the small bag out to me. I look from the bag to his face. He bought me the typewriter ornament.

Taking the bag from him, I just stand here. In my spot. Not talking.

And he's walking away.

"Chop chop lady, we're burning daylight."

Chapter 14

Todd

I know my car is a beater. I get shit about it from people all the time, but I don't care. I have no monthly payment, it gets me from points A to B safely, and you can't beat the gas mileage. Yes, I've had to invest in repairs here and there, but for the most part, this finely tuned machine barely counts toward my living expenses.

Plus, it has a kick-ass sound system. I made sure of that when I bought it ten years ago off a guy in town who was tired of it and wanted to unload it for something new. I'm sure he regrets it now, seeing as he's on his third car including payments since then and I'm still cruising along.

There's nothing sweeter than rolling with my homies through town, my man JT cryin' me a river while the bass pounds through the sub-woofer. Or something like that. I don't really know what a sub-woofer does. The only downside is I have to wear this throwback earpiece to talk hands-free. The sacrifices of winter driving, I look like a schmuck, but I have both hands on the wheel making death much less imminent for mountain driving.

No matter. Donna is enjoying herself and that's the whole point of this expedition. I can see she's struggling with some big decisions about her career, and maybe even some personal ones as well. Knowing she's been relaxing for the last few hours and really enjoying herself has put another notch on my man card, which I've needed after all the overly-sensitive emotional talk that's been going on inside my brain recently. Damn Aggi and her addictive story lines.

Unfortunately for me, between songs my phone alerts me of yet another call.

"Todd, I notice you haven't touched your food yet." "I don't eat meat or fish." "He's a homo."

I look over to see Donna staring at me, one eyebrow cocked.

"What?" I ask, trying to keep my eyes facing forward on the road, her to my right, and my phone resting in the cupholder all at once. It's a challenge but I'm that good.

"Really? You have that scene from *Wedding Crashers* as your ringtone?"

My own eyebrows shoot up in surprise. "You know *Wedding Crashers*?"

"It's one of my favorite movies," she says, turning to look out the window. "Owen Wilson and Vince Vaughn are hysterical together."

"I think I just fell in love," I mutter, making Donna laugh. How is this woman not in a serious relationship? Are all the pretty boys completely blind? Before my thoughts turn into words that might make her uncomfortable, I tap the button on my earpiece. "Well, hello, Marge."

She chuckles a throaty sound indicative of two decades of smoking. Marge is proud she quit last year. Pretty sure the Nicorette people were, too, when their stock skyrocketed from all her nicotine gum purchases.

"Hello, boss. What have you been up to lately?"

I glance over at Donna who suddenly has a death grip on the oh-shit handle as she looks back and forth between the road and me as I drive. I give her a quizzical look to which she responds, "Keep your eyes on the road! I don't want to die!"

Rolling my eyes I turn my attention back to Marge and the road ahead. It's been a long time since I've had a passenger in the winter that isn't used to the weather. If I didn't think she'd have a full-blown panic attack, I'd borrow a SUV and take her out on a few roads that aren't as plowed as ours.

I wouldn't have answered the call if the roads were even remotely slippery. They aren't. Cars and trucks coming up and down the mountain along with the bright sun help melt the plowed roads, making it just like any other day for driving. I should probably say something to Donna, explain that just because she's cold doesn't mean the roads are icy. Or that death is imminent. I could tell her about whiteouts and taking a turn too fast, spinning out on black ice. But, by the look on her face I don't think that would do her any good. Also, I'm far too entertained with her right now.

Answering Marge, I say, "Playing tour guide to a scaredy-cat."

Donna smacks me on the arm, which is a terribly unsafe thing to do when you are afraid of how someone drives, while Marge laughs again. "Must be an out-of-towner. They always freak out when it snows."

"This is why you work for me, Marge. You understand me completely."

"Which is how I know that before I give you a reminder"—I groan because if she's calling me to remind me of something, it's going to be important—"I need to update you on the office first."

"Always appreciate it when you start with good news. Hit me."

Marge spends the next few minutes giving me the rundown. The open house over the weekend resulted in a bidding war for my newest team member. I knew she was a good person to bring on. Selling the house for twenty-thousand over asking price is not too shabby, even in a resort town like this one. We've picked up two new listings in as many days, both priced over $500K, and four closings are scheduled for next week.

"For the off-season, I'd say that's pretty damn good," I praise.

"More than good. It's only February. By spring break, things will pick up even more, so I'm keeping an eye on a couple more agents you may want to consider bringing on."

"Especially if the college follows through with the plan to expand the sports complex. I'm anticipating an explosion of rentable properties on the market once that starts."

"I'm on the same page with you," she says, once again proving why I hired her in the first place. Marge understands the real estate market in this area like no one else. Why she never pursued her agent's license is beyond me, but as long as she's happy being my assistant, I can work with it. "Speaking of the convention center . . ."

I groan. The lightbulb in my brain turns on and I know what she's about to say.

"You realize you are the keynote speaker at the Idaho State Realtors Convention in about three hours, right?"

"Why do you sign me up for these things, Marge? Why do you hate me?"

"No way, buddy. I'm not taking the blame for this one. You know better than to check your work email after margarita night on Taco Tuesday. I'm still curious how many typos were in your response to the organizers when you agreed to this speech. And how much salsa ended up on the keypad."

"It was whiskey sours that night."

"You remember that, but you couldn't remember how to say no?"

Indicating with my blinker, I turn the car onto the narrow road through the trees that will lead us right to the cabin. It doesn't go unnoticed that Donna finally relaxes now that she can't see down a mountain while driving. City girl.

"That is not the point and you know it, Marge." She tries to interrupt with a "Mm-hmm," but I ignore her as I continue. "Moving on, though, if I'm going to make it on time, I'm gonna need you to send a car to get me at the cabin."

Because I haven't written my speech yet. But I know better than to tell her that.

"Already done. It'll be there in an hour."

"What? How did you know I'd be here?"

Marge's laugh is a little too loud this time. I'd write her up for being insubordinate or something, but that would make her laugh harder and then she'd tell my mother. It's not worth the effort. "You forget how small this town can be. I've gotten at least three phone calls today from friends who saw you shopping this morning. I hear she's real pretty."

I look at Donna out of the corner of my eye, pretending this conversation didn't just veer her direction. Besides, they're all wrong. Donna isn't pretty. She's the most beautiful woman I've ever met. And not just because of her looks.

Of course I don't say that to Marge, either. Again, she has my mother on speed dial. I'm already anticipating the third degree after she gets back from her cruise.

"Nosy busybodies need to mind their own business." Even though we all know some things will never change. "But I'm almost at the cabin now. I'll be ready in an hour. Oh hey, do you know if my navy suit is still in the back closet?"

"Yep. I had it delivered there last week. And Todd?

Whatever you do, do *not* wear the tie you bought from Marcy."

I scoff. "But it's my favorite. It has tiny little alligators that say 'bite me' on it."

"Exactly. This is a professional gathering. Get your businessman persona on and kill it, baby. You're already on their radar after being one of the top five brokers in the region and the top ten in the state over the last year alone. You can pretend to be as power hungry as they are for a couple hours."

I sigh because she's right. I love my job. I have built my business from the ground up and have a fantastic team under me, which allows me to work whatever hours I want. Our reputation is spreading far and wide and I've already started looking into expanding into other states. In some ways, I live a very charmed life. If turning into "Business Professional Todd" for a couple hours is my biggest sacrifice, I could be doing a hell of a lot worse.

Still, pulling up the driveway, I can't help but feel a little disappointed that I won't be spending the rest of the day here. I was having way too much fun with Donna. Oh well. Eventually it would have come to an end anyway. Right?

"All right, you've made your point." Putting the car into park, I let the engine run for the rest of the conversation. Donna just sits there. I'm not sure what she's waiting for, but I don't mind sitting next to her before I get back to reality. "I'm back now so I need to wash off my natural charm and glam it up for a bunch of suits."

"Good boy. Give me a call when it's over."

She hangs up, not even bothering to say goodbye. That's one of the great things about Marge. She doesn't waste my time with random pleasantries. She's fun to talk to but if it's not a) funny or b) the point of the conversation, she's out.

Dropping my phone in the center console, I let Donna in on our change of plans. "That was the boss."

She looks at me quizzically. "From the conversation, I thought that was your assistant or something."

"Same job, different title. She keeps me on track most of the time, so she can refer to herself however she wants."

"Good point." She laughs lightly but it doesn't reach her eyes. I may be seeing things, but I think Donna may have deduced the situation and is as disappointed as I am that I have to leave. Or I could have had one too many Irish coffee truffles from *Mountaintop Confections* and be having some wishful thinking.

"So obviously I got called into work."

"They did give you the morning to hang out with me. At some point they were going to need you back." She says it with a smile, but again . . . that Irish coffee is messing with me.

"Are you going to be okay? You seem a little nervous."

"Don't worry about me. I'll be just fine. You taught me how to rough it overnight if the power goes out again. Plus, I need to work and I'm feeling pretty inspired right now. Shouldn't be hard to crank out a few thousand words now that I've been enlightened on small-town living."

I nod, still feeling a small pit in my stomach because our time together is over. Turning off the engine, we head inside . . . Donna to the living room to write, me to the bedroom to transform into Professional Todd.

Chapter 15

Donna

Work. Todd has to go to work. Of course he does. It's a workday for most people and he's taken half the day to play tour guide to me. While I appreciate his sacrifice, guilt has nudged at me all day too. I've had a lot of friendships change over the years after leaving a traditional nine to five job in lieu of writing full time. My schedule, as much as I try to keep one, isn't really a schedule at all.

If I'm out with a girlfriend and an idea for a scene of my current work in progress or a new story pops in my head, I will usually have to pause our conversation and type notes into my phone. I've even written entire chapters on my phone during a movie. I admit I was surprised that the threat of being kicked out of a movie for being on your phone is just that—a threat. It worked to my advantage, though. Because in my line of work, new ideas and new scenes are what butter my bread so to speak. If I don't get the thoughts down as soon as they come to me, they may be lost forever. Like socks in the dryer.

Where do those go anyway? I've heard they re-incarnate as Tupperware lids that have no matching bowls.

Also, I'm easily distracted. I was never like this in my former attorney life. I was structured and disciplined, never late and never without all my ducks in a row. Now that my full-time job is one of creativity, and I'm actually encouraged to take breaks, step away from my work to think, I have discovered some of the most ridiculous time sucks.

Trash television? Check. Level 476 of a game on my phone? Double check. Online videos of cats shaking their tails to music? Super check. I do that every day. Don't even get me started on social media. That is the biggest time sucks of them all but also one of the most vital parts of my business. Oprah has no idea how lucky she is to have started building her empire before the days of posts, likes, and comments.

I've also become used to being on my own, spending my days chatting on the phone with an author friend or two and updating my social media accounts. That's why today was so nice. It was fun to spend time with another adult, albeit one with a teenage sense of humor, and have real conversations. I laughed. I laughed a lot. Truthfully, I'm concerned about the status of my cheeks. A trip to an esthetician for a face massage may need to take place sooner rather than later.

While my tour guide changes into his work clothes, which I can only imagine include a pair of khakis and a polo shirt with the name of real estate office he works for stitched above his heart, I open my gift. The small typewriter is wrapped in bright red tissue paper and although I've seen it, a little flutter of excitement ripples through me. Slowly, I reveal the ornament and I can't help the smile that takes over my face. My heart is full as I realize this ornament will sit on my tree, or my desk because I doubt I'll put it away without reminding me of today with Todd.

A throat clearing startles me from my thoughts.

Holy. Shit.

Those aren't khakis.

Standing in the entry way to the living room is a gorgeous man dressed in a suit that if I were to guess, costs somewhere in the four-digit range. Dark navy, the perfectly tailored suit accentuates parts of Todd's body I didn't know existed. Broad shoulders, a tapered waist, and thighs that could easily crack a walnut.

Wow, he wasn't kidding about the temperature heating up. Only, I don't think it's this thick sweater I'm wearing, but the man standing before me, that has my skin flushed. He's adjusting the sleeves of his shirt under the suit coat when his eyes lift and meet mine.

Swallowing the lump that has formed in my throat, I openly stare at him. I should be embarrassed by my reaction. I should not be thinking about slipping my hands under that coat and pulling it off his shoulders before I slowly unbutton his shirt and . . . okay at this point there would be no slowly unbuttoning anything. I'd channel one of my lead characters and rip that bitch open just so I can run my hands up his pecs.

Dear God. I'm having a sexual fantasy about Todd.

Not Hawk Weaver. Not the recently named Sexiest Man Alive. Todd. The man who has shown me kindness, friendship, and encouraged me to do what makes me happy and not what is expected.

I have a mad crush on a man who wears questionable shirts most days while practicing his method acting. He isn't the type of man I meet on my dating app. He's the opposite. Yet, as he stands before me, he isn't. He's sexier than any of the corporate executives I've gone out with since, well . . . maybe ever.

How did I not see this plot twist coming?

Opening my mouth to say something, I'm cut short when his phone rings. Instead of the previous quote from my favorite movie, it's a standard ring tone. Tilting my head to the side as he raises his finger to stop me from saying anything, he answers the call.

"Hello? Oh, good afternoon, Charles. Yes, I did have a chance to review your proposal and while I appreciate the offer, you and I both know it is far below asking." Todd walks toward the wall of windows as he listens to the man on the other side of the call, shoving one hand in his pocket, which stretches the material of his fitted jacket a little tighter over his ass. What is happening here?

"I don't disagree, but you know me well enough to know I will not call my client when your offer is nothing short of offensive. Speak with your buyer and give me a call when you aren't three below asking."

And my panties are soaked. Todd is a boss. I don't think he's literally a boss but, in that suit, speaking with authority, and holding himself with such confidence, I'm turned on beyond belief. I guess Clara was right. I do have a type, and he's not only what I write, but he's also come to life right before my eyes.

"Sorry about that," he says, pulling me from my quickly turning dirty thoughts.

"Oh . . . uh . . ." I stammer, never really saying anything at all. That's when I notice his tie is a mess. I don't know how it's possible, but the imperfection makes him even sexier. It makes him more—Todd.

Slowly, I walk toward him, his eyes narrowing in confusion. I step up in front of him and raise my hands to his tie. The moment my hands touch the silky fabric, his body stiffens.

"Who taught you how to tie a tie? This is a mess." The raspiness of my voice is not lost on me.

Instead of responding, Todd places his hand on top of mine. My eyes lift to meet his and as cheesy and fake as it sounds, time stops. I hear nothing around us except the beating of my heart in my ears.

"You don't have to—"

"I want to," I say, cutting him off. Before I can fix it, the shapes on his tie focus into pictures, and I can't help but smile. "Todd, why are there alligators that say 'bite me' on your tie?"

"Don't tell Marge," he whispers. I smile again because even in his power suit, he makes no apologies for who he is. It's endearing and oddly sexy.

Slowly, I adjust his tie so it isn't halfcocked to the side and the pattern askew. Thinking of the word cock suddenly sends a volt of sexual awareness through me.

Todd's hand slides from where it rests on my hand up my arm and then down my side, coming to rest on my hip.

Satisfied with the status of his tie, I slowly run my hand down the soft fabric, settling it on his waist. Our eyes connect, and I wait for a count of three, giving him an opportunity to make a move. Okay it was more a count of two before I rise to my toes and place my lips on his.

Warm soft lips kiss me back and when his tongue nudges the seam of them open, I give myself to him fully. His arms envelope me and my hands link behind his neck. I'm not a young girl and have had my share of first kisses. The first being in the fifth grade on a dare with Tommy Angelino. It wasn't the greatest first kiss, but it sure beat some of the others as I got older. Don't get me started on the high school jocks. Sloppy is being kind.

But this. This first kiss with Todd, it is slow and sensual. Strong and powerful. Promising and hopeful. We kiss for what feels like an eternity but when he pulls back, his hand lifting to cup my cheek, it feels too short.

With a soft peck to my lips, my eyes flutter open, looking up at him through my lashes where a smile greets me. "That was unexpected." Shyly, I smile and look down. "Don't be embarrassed."

"I'm not embarrassed," I mumble.

Before he can respond, his phone chimes in his pocket and he lets out a long sigh. "That's my car. Will you be okay here while I'm gone?"

Nodding I ask, "What exactly do you do, Todd?"

"I sell houses."

"Dressed in this?" I ask, running my finger across the lapel of his suit coat.

Chuckling he steps out of our embrace, and I already miss his hands on me. "Not always. Today I have to play the part and talk to a group of stiffs about the market and what I project is coming in the next year."

"Wow. You're quite a mystery, aren't you?"

Leaving me standing in my spot, he makes it to the door and turns to me. "I'll be back in a few hours. Don't go anywhere."

As the door closes behind him, I say to only myself, "Not a chance in hell."

When Todd left for his meeting, I had no idea what to do with myself. I was wound up tight, my hormones running rampant. I contemplated a bath and a nap. I'm on vacation after all. But, instead, I sat down at the dining table, powered up my laptop, and . . . wrote. I wrote for hours, never stopping. The words flowed from my fingertips like they never have. Even my first book didn't come to me as seamless as this one.

The sweet romance. The one book my agent will kill me for submitting. It's also the only book in two years that has made me feel like I may actually have something great happening.

My highest word count in a single day was eleven

thousand and I sacrificed a lot that day. Mostly, sleep, food, and relaxed muscles. Today though, as I look at the lower left-hand corner of my computer screen, I see that if I keep this up for a few more hours, I will surpass that goal.

Allowing myself a ten-minute break, I rise from the table and use the restroom before heading to the kitchen for something to drink. Glancing at the clock on the microwave, I am at that awkward part of the afternoon. I've missed a reasonable lunch hour and am hours from dinner. Opening the refrigerator, I see the blocks of cheese from Todd's awful attempt at snacks from last night and smile and pull the block from its perch along with a bowl of grapes.

Once I've put together a little plate of cheese, crackers, and grapes, I pour myself a glass of iced tea and return to my work. Immersing myself into the story, I polish off the plate of food and suck down my tea without realizing it.

I'm not sure how much time has passed, but soon the sun is setting, and the room begins to darken. Since I'm at a good stopping point in the story, I click the save button and close my laptop. Standing from the table, I eye the fireplace and pile of wood nestled next to it. I'm an independent woman. I can easily build a fire by myself. Contemplating exactly how one goes about starting a fire, I do what any modern woman does. I open my laptop and consult the internet.

Twenty minutes and only a few mishaps later, I am nestled on the couch, wrapped in a blanket with the fire roaring before me, and one of Todd's recorded episodes of *The Voice* on the television. Completely engrossed in the performance on the screen, I don't hear anyone come in, but when he whispers in my ear, I do what I attempted last night. Smack him right in the head.

"Holy shit!"

"Ohmygod I'm so sorry," I shout, jumping up and turning to face him. Todd is standing behind the couch, jacket off, tie loosened at the neck, and sleeves of his shirt rolled up to his elbows. Ladies, I can confirm that my panties are official gone. Poof. Gone. Nothing left to see here. Holy hotness.

"I thought you heard me come in."

Shaking my head, I walk around the couch to where he's standing, his hand covering his eye. Slowly, I reach up and remove his hand and cringe when I see the red mark on his face.

"I am so sorry, Todd. I think it's going to leave a bruise."

"It's okay, I hear chick's dig a guy who looks like he's been in a fight."

Laughing I ask, "Is that so? Well, I must say, it does scream *bad boy*."

Todd looks to the television and raises a single brow at me before shaking his head and smiling. Busted. "You started a fire."

For some reason, his realization that I did something completely out of my wheelhouse makes me a little embarrassed. Suddenly very interested in my fingernails, I mutter, "I did. I hope that was okay."

Taking my hand in his, he says, "It's absolutely okay. I want you to be comfortable here. I'm going to change. Have you eaten?"

"Just a little snack."

"How about I change and then we make dinner? If you're okay with it, we can finish this episode together."

Smiling, I nod in agreement. Squeezing my hand, he walks away and down the hall. Me? I fan myself because it isn't just the fire making me a little hot tonight.

Chapter 16

Todd

It feels so good to be out of that monkey suit. I know it's part of the gig and all, but it's so stifling to have to tone down my personality. Especially since very few people attending the conference will reach the level of success I have. That's not being cocky, that's fact. While we all have access to the same information—the current market, projected changes in the market, a house's marketability—I seem to have a little secret weapon. Me. There is more to this industry than being knowledgeable. When it comes to working with clients, the number one thing you have to have is the ability to make them relax. To enjoy the process.

Let's face it . . . buying a house is stressful. Selling a house is stressful. My job isn't only to reach whatever goal they have, it's also to keep them sane during the process. Being down-to-earth and go with the flow is exactly what most of my clients need.

It's also what most agents don't have. But what they always have is a well-pressed suit, which is my least favorite part of the job. Thank goodness I have a fully stocked closet here with everything I need to dress up and play the part.

That reminds me—at some point I need to ask Marge why the hell I have a fully stocked closet here with a bunch of my clothes and one very expensive suit. I assume she had some hand in it. I doubt I would have forgotten something like half my wardrobe. Or, maybe in my hastiness to move to my next flip project, I left them behind. Stranger things have happened.

Either way, it's serving me well tonight.

Meandering into the kitchen, Donna is pulling ingredients out of the pantry. I admit, I wasn't positive how she'd react to my return after the conference. I took a guess that she'd be fine with me infiltrating her vacation again, especially after that super-hot kiss. Still not sure what that was all about.

Must have been the suit.

Huh. Maybe I should wear them more often. Between that and the voice, I'm a bigger babe magnet than I realized.

"Finding everything you're looking for?"

Donna glances over her shoulder, a sultry look on her face. She opens her mouth to respond when she stops and her expression completely changes. "Really," she deadpans, "you're wearing unicorns tonight?"

Aaaand sarcastic Donna is back.

"What's wrong with unicorns?" I smooth down the cotton blend, painfully aware that she's no longer looking at me like I'm her next meal. Damn. "Unicorns are magical creatures who live on rainbows and shit ice cream."

"Shit ice cream?"

My eyes widen. "Please tell me you've seen that internet commercial for the Squatty Potty."

A small laugh comes out of her as she drops a bag of pasta, a jar of Alfredo sauce and an onion on the counter. "The what?"

"Where do I find these poor, unworldly people," I mutter, my hand running down my face. "The Squatty Potty. It's the world's best spoof commercial ever, for a product that actually exists."

"I'll have to take your word for it," she says as she rifles through the drawers, not finding what she's looking for.

"One of these days, woman, I'm going to sit you down and give you the complete education of Todd's world. You will never be the same."

"Somehow, I don't doubt you."

She's still rifling so I walk around the giant island, opening the drawer next to her and pulling out the best vegetable cutting knife known to man. Presenting it to her I ask, "Is this what you're looking for?"

Smiling brightly, she takes it from me. "Yes. Thank you. Do you mind heating up a pan to sauté the onion? I know you got us ready-made sauce, but I'd like to add some onion for flavor."

"Sure. I'll do ya one better and fill a pot with water to start the pasta as well."

"You're a good man."

She begins the task of chopping the onion and I make a personal wager on how long until she starts crying from the fumes. My best guess is ninety seconds. Starting now.

"What did you have to do for work today anyway?" I'm not sure if she's really interested in my job or if she's just making conversation. It's not really that exciting. Especially this part.

"It was the Idaho State Realtors Association. They have a convention every year and this time it's being held at the local college."

"Did you learn a lot?"

"Oh, I wasn't attending. I was the keynote speaker."

The room goes quiet except for me putting the pan on the stove and turning on the burner. When a few seconds pass and she doesn't say anything, I turn around.

Donna's frozen in place, knife resting on top of the onion, and nowhere near getting teary eyed. I may have misjudged her.

"What?" I finally ask before we once again fall into a staring contest. It would be very embarrassing for her to lose twice.

She looks back and forth like she's trying to get two separate ideas to make sense. "You were the keynote speaker?"

"Uh, yeah?"

Placing the knife on the chopping block, she turns and leans against the counter, arms crossed. I have no idea what is happening here, but it could go any number of ways.

"Todd. What exactly do you do for a living?"

"I work in real estate."

"Nuh-uh. There's more to it than that."

"I'm not sure what you mean." I totally know what she means.

"You take time off whenever you want, you own this"—she gestures around the room—"amazing piece of property. You have an assistant and you were the keynote speaker at the Idaho State Realtors Convention."

"Right. I work in real estate."

She stomps her foot in frustration, and I know the jig is up. "Come on, Todd. You're holding out on me. Give me a job title."

I sigh and lean against the counter. "Fine. I own my own firm."

"I knew it!"

I can't help the massive eye roll that crosses my face. "You did not."

"Well no. Not until just now. But you're a business genius, aren't you?"

"Define genius."

"If I had to guess, I'd say you have a team of at least a dozen under you, you were probably listed as a top seller in your region, if not your state, and you probably bought this cabin originally to flip it, and then realized you could make a better profit by holding onto it and using it as a rental property instead."

Now it's my turn to stare wide-eyed. "How did you know all that?"

She shrugs and turns back to her onion. "I've spent the last several years researching different kinds of businesses and the people who run them. Once the pieces of the puzzle come together, it's not that hard to figure out."

"Dammit, I blew my cover," I mutter. "I should have dressed down more often."

Donna barks out a laugh and scrapes a few of the onion slices into her palms and dumps them in the pan. "Don't underestimate yourself. Your crazy shirts are what threw me off in the first place."

"Success!"

She shakes her head. "You're crazy, ya know that?"

"That's why you like me."

She pauses for a second before picking up her knife and working on the onion again. "Yeah. Yeah, I think it is."

I hate to admit defeat, but Donna was right. Adding some chopped onion made my favorite go-to Alfredo sauce that much better. Not that we were trying to do anything fancy. Just two people enjoying each other's company over the comfort of cheesy pasta.

We were both so full we didn't bother with the

dishes. Just tossed them in some hot water in the sink knowing we'll regret the decision later, but whatever. The alternative was, well . . . doing dishes.

Instead, we made our way to the couch to catch up on more episodes of The Voice. Those plans were thwarted, however, when Donna got some random idea she called a plot bunny, whatever that means, and grabbed her laptop right in the middle of the judges arguing over a contestant. Considering that's her favorite part, I knew this new rabbit had to be important. I can only assume it's a story about a pet owner.

I've spent the last few hours trying to watch the remaining episodes of *The Voice* while she works, but it isn't the same without her. The way she's abusing the keys of her laptop, I assume she's onto a really great idea. Or ideas. I mean, it is bunnies and you know what they say about them multiplying. Giving up my quest to absorb all the southern greatness Blake has to offer, I mute the television and grab my laptop. I should check in with the office and ensure everything is on track for our next closing. A quick scroll through my emails and a series of texts to my junior brokers, I connect my earbuds and settle into the couch.

Eyeing the almost empty glass of wine on the table, I wonder if Donna will continue to nurse the single glass or just finish it. She's been alternating between typing at lightning speed and staring off into space with her wine glass perched to her lips, only an occasional sip here and there. It's like the aroma of liquid is fueling her creative juices. I have no room to talk; I'm easily distracted by a squirrel on a branch outside the window, so whatever works for her.

Placing my tongue up against the back of my teeth, I press my lips together and then force them into a tight "o" position. Carefully blowing through my teeth, I let out a shrill whistle. I think it sounds almost identical to the one I've been listening to for the last ten minutes.

I don't know for sure though because Donna just threw a pillow at my head, knocking my ear bud out.

"Why are you throwing shit at me, woman?"

"Why are you making shrill whistling sounds? You scared the shit out of me."

I roll my eyes and scoff. "I'm not making whistling sounds, Donna. I'm learning the language of my native people."

She does this weird rapid eye-blinking thing that probably means she's trying to decide if I'm lying or just making shit up as I go.

"Seriously. It's a real thing."

"Whistling is the language of your native people." It's a statement not a question. She's processing my words and still looking at me like I'm the one who's confused.

Determined to show her how cool this actually is, I click out of the program I'm using and do a quick Google search.

"Here," I say, turning my laptop toward her.

"Turkish Whistling, also known as Bird Language is a series of high-pitched whistles used by some remote villages to communicate over large distances," she reads aloud. "An endangered language with only about ten thousand speakers worldwide, it's now making a comeback and is being taught in some schools." She looks at me like it's the most fascinating things she's ever read. "You're learning an endangered bird language?"

"It's actually a people language but yes. I am." Turning my laptop back, I click out of the article and back into the program.

"But why?"

"Why not?" I ask with a shrug. "I like knowing things. Especially obscure things most people don't know. Not trivia, per se. Just stuff that might not seem important when you find out about it, but when you look closer, it's unique."

Donna leans forward and picks up her wine glass, tipping to her mouth and before taking a sip she says, "I love that. Love that you see the value where others might miss it."

"Yeah well. It also makes it easier to communicate with Bill, my building manager, instead of having to go outside in the snow and up the stairs. I'm making him learn it too."

Thankfully she hadn't actually gotten the wine glass to her lips because she started laughing. Plus, I'm not a cabernet man and being covered in it after she spits it all over me doesn't sound like fun.

"Anyway, are you finally at a stopping point on your book?"

Smiling, she stretches her arms over her head. "I

think I actually am."

"Good!" I pop up from the couch and head to the kitchen to gather supplies. When I come back, I hand her the already opened bottle of wine and keep the ice-cold pale ale for myself. "Let's play a drinking game."

Placing both our laptops on the far end of the coffee table, she takes the bottle I'm handing her and twists the top off, filling the rest of her glass to the top. "What kind of drinking game are we talking about?"

"Let's keep with our musical marathon. Every time a judge turns around before the song is over, we drink."

Donna quirks one eyebrow up. "That could end up being a lot of drinks in a row."

I shrug. "Could be. Or we could remain woefully sober. We don't know how good the contestants are yet, do we?"

She pretends to be weighing her options, but I can tell what her answer is going to be. Finally, she's caves.

"You're on."

We clink our drinks and I grab the remote, ready for a night of drunken competition.

Chapter 17

Donna

Giant fireballs burn my eyes.

Giant fireballs?

That can't be right. Carefully I pry my eyelids open. It's a little bit of a struggle considering my lashes are stuck together. With one eye open, I look around the room. Ever so slowly because there is currently a marching band playing the worst rock song known to mankind in my head. If I were to guess, I'd say the entire percussion section has crawled into my head and declared it their new home.

Holy mother of all hangovers. I should have known this would happen. Two bottles of red wine and hours of banter, laughter, and nothing but roasted marshmallows for sustenance can only lead to this level of ick. Sliding my tongue across my teeth I cringe at what I feel—furriness. Moaning quietly, I continue to scan my surroundings and stiffen when I feel a warm hand wrapped around my waist, a stiff body behind me. By body I mean part. Body part.

Todd.

Memories of last night flood my mind like a hurricane and a wave of nausea hits me. Uncertain if it's from the leftover wine or realization I'm spooning with one of my best friend's best friends and a man I hardly know, I slowly inhale and exhale, hoping to ward off the need to run for the toilet.

Last night our drinking game quickly turned into more of a game of truth. No dares here, just simple truths. What our childhoods were like, who we wanted to be when we were growing up—a badass modern version of Wonder Woman for me and a train conductor for Todd—and most of all, where we want to be a few years from now. I learned that while on the surface he jokes and wears silly shirts, deep down Todd is kind, giving, and supportive of those in his life. It doesn't matter to him if he's known you twenty years or twenty minutes, he'd give you the shirt off his back if he thought it would help.

His success in real estate sort of happened on a whim, and since major financial success was never something he dreamed of, he's continued to live his life the same way he did growing up. Of course, when he does indulge, he takes it to the extreme. Yes, parked outside is a twenty-year-old car that probably costs more to maintain than it is worth, but he owns over six homes or buildings currently under construction. He invests in real estate and investments that will grow and allow him to provide jobs and futures for people, instead of on materialistic things like high-end name-brand clothing and cars.

The body wrapped around mine begins to shift, and I freeze, not wanting to wake him if he's still sleeping.

Too late.

Lips are pressed to my neck and goosebumps cover my skin. Memories of last night and him kissing me on the lips, the neck, the shoulder—below my shoulder, aka my boobs—multiply those goosebumps. The way he made me feel with each graze of his lips sends my heart racing.

"Mornin', beautiful."

Smiling, I rasp, "Good morning."

"The next time I build a house from the ground up, remind me to demand curtains."

Laughing, I roll onto my back, careful to keep my face out of his line of breathing. I'm sure my breath is beyond anything sexy. Stretching my hands over my head and pointing my toes, I note Todd hasn't removed his arm from where it's flung across my stomach.

"Or we could have slept in one of the many beds in this house." I pause as the words tumble from my mouth. "I mean, we could have each slept in a bed . . ."

Laughing, Todd says, "I like beds. But I like lying with you just as much." He places another quick kiss to my shoulder. Something else I learned last night was how once he was given the green light, he was always touching me. Pinkies linked, hand on my knee, lips on my own. Always in contact.

Clara would tease me for days if she knew how much I loved it. The way his simple gestures warm my heart and make me feel like a giddy teenager is nothing I'm used to, but somehow, exactly what I've been missing. The men I've dated are more about appearances, excessive fucking, and keeping PDA to a minimum, and of course, after my last couple of dates, at least one that could be attributed to him having a wife.

"What do you want to do today?" Todd asks, scooting closer to me, his embrace tightening.

"Oh, I figured I'd write. I'm sure you have things to do." *Keep it casual, Donna.* Do not let him know you secretly hope he plans to spend his day here. Not whistling, of course. I could do without that distraction.

"Not a thing on my calendar. What would you say to playing hooky today? Just hanging out and doing nothing."

"Isn't that what we've been doing?" I ask, turning my attention to him. Eyes wide, he opens and closes his mouth like a fish on a hook.

My breath. It's my morning breath. I knew it was bad enough to melt paint, but he doesn't need to be so obvious. I begin to pull away from him but before I can make it far, Todd licks the tip of his thumb and then . . . wipes under my eye.

"Eww, what the heck?" I shout, swatting his hand away.

"Babe, it looks like you are planning your Halloween costume and Rocky Racoon is your only option."

Sitting up quickly, I continue to bat his hands away as he tries to pull me back down. Mimicking his move of wetting my fingers with my tongue, I quickly wipe away any makeup that has settled under my eyes. The sound of his deep laugh have an effect on me, and I relax a little but still swat his hands away.

"Don't you know you can't make fun of a woman and her morning-after makeup?" I scold.

"Sorry. I tried to help, but you, once again, channeled the Karate Kid. So, what do you say? A Todd day? Relaxation, popcorn, and maybe a movie marathon. Pants optional."

Shrugging, I feign contemplation before his fingers dig into my side and begin tickling me. Laughing, I fall back onto to my pillow and look into his chocolate-colored eyes. While I was laughing, Todd found a way to nestle himself between my legs, his arms resting on either side of my head. Lips sealed tight, I stare at him, waiting for his next move.

And he stares right back. Another standoff. This has quickly become our thing and while I'd love nothing more than to win this round, the pressure of him on my bladder has me lifting myself up, placing a quick kiss to his lips. Stunned, he slips in his stance, and I toss him onto his back.

"First, bathroom, shower, and some breakfast," I declare as I scurry from the living room and down the hall to the master bathroom.

Another interesting tidbit about my new friend—he likes a good musical. I'll admit I'm not normally a huge fan of musical theater but watching the modern versions with Todd has been both enlightening and fun. His commentary and behind the scenes knowledge are like a front row seat to a critic and historian. Although, like with his television show, he has fancied himself a singer and I have reminded him he is not. My ears thank me for stopping him with a series of kisses ten minutes ago when he channeled his inner Hugh Jackman. Why couldn't he be like most men and insist we watch an action movie? The answer to that question is simple, Todd Chimolski isn't most men.

"I like this take-charge version of you," he mumbles on my lips, his hands resting on my hips as I lean into him.

Rolling my eyes, I run my fingers through the hair at the nape of his neck before laying my lips on his again. Deepening the kiss, I let him control the intensity. Slow and intense is how Todd kisses. He doesn't know it but this kiss, this weekend, will be featured in one of my books sooner rather than later.

A loud rumble sounds from his stomach and I giggle, "I could eat too."

"How about one of my signature grilled cheese sandwiches?"

"Signature?" I ask, sitting back on his lap.

Smacking my ass lightly, he stands, picking me up with him and gently setting my feet on the ground. "Come with me and prepare to be amazed. I make a mean grilled cheese."

I follow him into the kitchen and take a spot at the breakfast bar while he begins pulling out the pans and ingredients for our lunch. We chit chat as he goes about preparing our food. I sip on a cup of hot tea and laugh at his attempt to tell stories while changing out his accents.

"I think you need to work on that Irish one a little more. It was a little less Irish and more Brooklyn sounding to me."

Throwing his hand over his heart dramatically he scoffs. I laugh. "I suppose you're right. This narrator life is harder than it looks. Or sounds. I suppose sounds is more appropriate. Your lunch, muh lady."

Picking up the offered sandwich, I smile in appreciation. If this sandwich tastes half as good as it smells, I may have to kidnap Todd and take him home with me. Biting into the crisp bread, the flavors of three different cheese burst in my mouth and I let out an exaggerated moan.

Pulled from my moment of euphoria, I look at Todd across the bar as he adjusts himself behind the counter. "Woman, you cannot make those sounds. I'm only so strong."

Winking, I repeat the sound and then take off running from my spot as he chases me. When his arms wrap around my waist, I let him turn me to face him and silence my laughter with his kisses. Until the sound of a key in the lock of the front door startles us both.

It's like a scratching record, and we pull apart, almost like our skin is on fire just as the one person we have in common steps through the doorway.

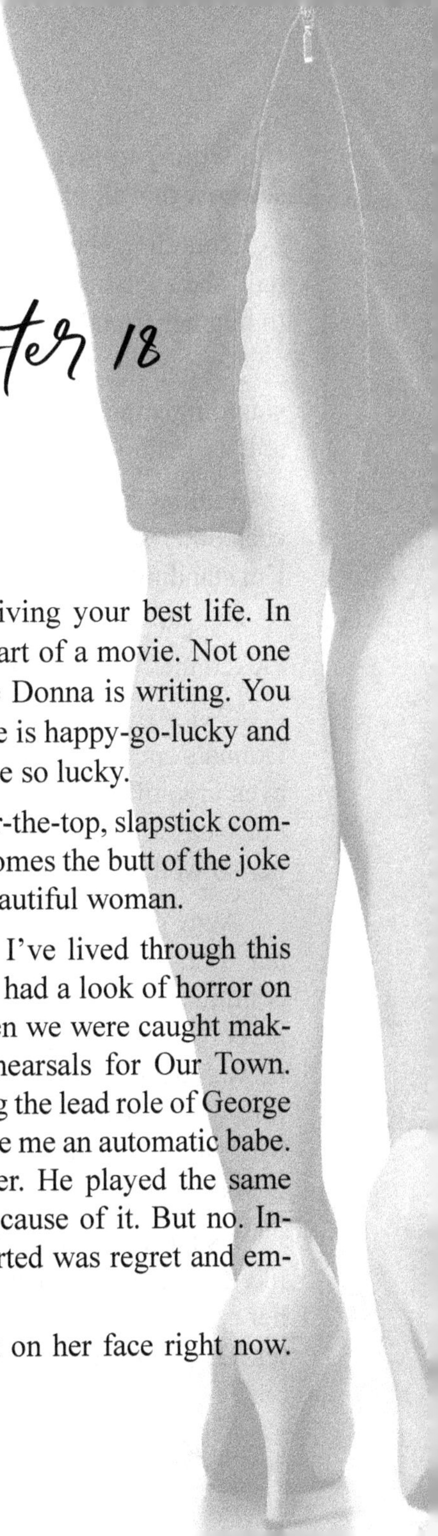

Chapter 18

Todd

This is not what you call living your best life. In fact, I'm pretty sure I'm part of a movie. Not one of those cheesy romances like Donna is writing. You know, the ones where everyone is happy-go-lucky and no one ever fights. I couldn't be so lucky.

Nope. It's one of those over-the-top, slapstick comedies where the nerdy guy becomes the butt of the joke when it comes to dating the beautiful woman.

Not that it's the first time I've lived through this particular script. Vicki Pantori had a look of horror on her face in eleventh grade when we were caught making out back stage during rehearsals for Our Town. Didn't matter that I was playing the lead role of George Gibbs, which should have made me an automatic babe. Just look at David Schwimmer. He played the same role and is a solid "seven" because of it. But no. Instead, the only look Vicki sported was regret and embarrassment.

Donna has that same look on her face right now.

I'm willing to give her the benefit of the doubt until I see how this all plays out.

Rounding the corner, Aggi drops her bag. "Donna!" she exclaims, tripping over said bag as she moves to hug her friend. "It's so good to see you!"

"What are you doing here?" Donna asks, still sounding stunned. And startled. Maybe regretful? I'm still assessing.

Pulling back, Aggi and Donna continue to hold each other's arms the way women do. In the meantime, I'm standing here, waiting to be noticed.

"Spencer's mother flew in last night. She basically kicked me out and sent me here for our girls' trip."

"What? You didn't need to leave him like that." Donna's speaking in compassionate sentences, but her eyes are still wild. I wonder if Aggi notices or if the only reason I can see it is because I've gotten to know her so well.

Aggi pulls away and pushes her dark hair out of her face. "Trust me. He's fine." Rolling her eyes, she continues, "He's being a big ole baby, and I told him he could have me now as a nursemaid or later when he was well. It helped that I reminded him the doctor forbid him from having any crazy sex until after the MRI at the earliest. So of course he opted for having me back later."

I stick my tongue out and make a gagging noise like I always do when Aggi mentions anything about her sex life. Because it's Aggi. She's basically my sister. Of course, that gagging sound is also what makes her finally notice me.

"Hey Todd. What are you doing here?" she asks as she hugs me quickly.

Just as I open my mouth to respond, Donna interjects. "The power went out."

My eyebrows shoot up in surprise at her response, while Aggi quickly looks around the room. "Um, the TV's on."

"It came back." Again, Donna with the quick answers. "Todd came over to check on me and made me some lunch. Wasn't that nice of him?"

Donna looks at me with pleading in her eyes. Like she's begging me not to say anything about how long I've really been here. About what has really been going on between us. About us at all.

Aggi, on the other hand, looks back and forth between us. I know her well enough to know she's not fooled. I also know her well enough to know she's not going to say anything about it.

Shoving my hands in my pockets, I clear my throat and briefly look at the ground before giving Donna what she wants—an out.

"Yep. But she's got it under control. Made it through the night and all that."

"I can see that," Aggi says, but I see the questions in her eyes. In Donna's, I see relief for joining her in her farce. For keeping the last three days a secret. I won't lie, that one stings.

"So yeah." I begin shuffling my way to the door.

"Now that you're here, Ags, I'm just gonna head on out." Refusing to make eye contact, I quickly pack up my laptop and phone, making sure to grab my keys.

Before she says anything, I feel Donna move closer to me. I'm not sure what to think about that. Five minutes ago it would have made my heart race and my mouth salivate. Now, now it kind of makes me want to vomit.

"You don't have to go, Todd," she says quietly, and I squeeze my eyes tight for a split second before standing straight and looking her dead in the eye. She's wringing her hands, but I don't even know what to make of that.

"Yeah, I think I do." Shooting my gaze around the room, I smile weakly at Aggi and then return my attention back to Donna. "You're in good hands. Besides, I've been lazy with some work stuff for the last couple of days. Money won't make itself, ya know."

I have no idea why I just said that. It doesn't even sound like me, but right now I don't exactly feel like me, either. All I know for sure is I want out of this place. I want away from this awkward situation. And I want to go lick my newfound emotional wounds.

"Anyway, it was good to see you, Donna. Bye, Ags."

Heading to the car, I don't even look behind me. Not when I close the door. Not when I walk down the stairs. Not even when I hear Aggi come out behind me.

"Todd?"

"Yeah." I don't turn around as I load my bag into

the passenger side of my car. I don't want her to see the emotions on my face, which I know full well she'll figure out immediately.

"Um, I don't know what I just walked into, but I know you didn't just show up to check on Donna."

Slamming the door, I walk around the front of my car to the driver's side. "Doesn't really matter, Ags."

"But it does, Todd." I continue to ignore her. "Todd!"

"What?" I blurt out, finally looking at her, one foot already in the car.

"This isn't like that time with Vicki Pantori in high school."

A humorless smirk crosses my face. "I know." Climbing into my car, I slam the door and crank the ignition. "It's worse," I say to myself as I drive away.

With nowhere I have to be and nothing I have to do, I keep my foot on the gas and just drive. And think.

I know I'm no one's eye candy. That's never been up for debate. But I'm some damn good ear candy, and I won't chase someone who can't recognize that.

Thinking over the last few days, I have to ask myself what exactly did Donna and I have anyway? It was three days of shopping and kissing and watching The Voice. Yes, it was the most fun three days I've had in a long time, but that doesn't make it a relationship. It doesn't make a commitment. Hell, it doesn't even really make a solid friendship.

No, three days makes a good time and some good

memories. If that's all Donna wants from it, can I fault her for that? No. There was never a discussion about what we were doing. She doesn't owe me anything. And realistically, even if she is as interested in me as I am in her, she lives in Arizona. I live in Idaho. How would something more than what we've already shared work?

It wouldn't. And as much as I pride myself on being an intellectual guy, it seems Donna is the smart one in this situation. She already knew what has taken me longer to process: the last three days have been a vacation fling. An incredible, life-altering, story-inspiring three days. Nothing more than that.

Taking a deep breath and blowing it back out, I try to shake off my hurt feelings. As much as it sucks, I need to let it go. If this is the worst thing to happen in my life, I'm doing pretty damn good. I just have to figure out how to be grateful for that.

Chapter 19

Donna

Game face on. I need to put on my best smile and calm my shit. And text Todd and apologize for being such a complete asshole. Why did I jump away from him like he was on fire? I acted like we'd been busted doing something wrong by one of our parents. I'm not a teenager, and this isn't my parents' home.

There is nothing wrong with what Todd and I were doing. Or about to do. If I'm being honest, and other than how I just behaved I usually am, it was headed for some much-needed relief and sexiness. I know it in my gut. I know that if Aggi hadn't walked in the door, if she hadn't interrupted us, we would have had sex. Hot, probably slightly award-winning, fulfilling sex.

I have no doubt about it. Sex with Todd would have been great. He's great. He's funny and kind, and I blew him off and pretended like he was none of those things. Because I'm a horrible person.

Defeated, I make my way to the kitchen and pour myself a glass of wine. Day drinking on vacation is absolutely acceptable and although last night was an overindulgence, I don't care. Today, the crisp white is going down with complete ease, and I pour myself another glass, this time a little less generous on the pour.

When the front door closes, I brace myself for what's to come. I'm sure it'll start with a sympathetic smile from Aggi, followed by an "I'm sorry," and then a "get your shit and get out, you hurt my best friend." I wouldn't blame her. Instead of moving, I stay planted in the same spot and sip my wine as she walks into the space.

"Hey, don't be stingy! Pour me a glass too." Nodding, I pull another glass from the cabinet and twist the cap off, filling her glass, and since it's silly to put so little back in the refrigerator, I pour the remainder in my glass.

Aggi and I both take a drink from our glass, an awkward silence settling between us.

"I'm just going to say this once and then you're going to tell me what the hell you're watching on the television. Okay?" I nod and sip. "I obviously walked in on something. I'm not certain if you were arguing or what but if Todd said something to upset you, I apologize." I open my mouth to speak but she doesn't stop to allow me. "Now, I also know Todd better than anyone else and know that isn't who he is. That being said, he's a good guy, Donna. Other than Spencer, the greatest blessing in my life. Oh and present company, of course."

"Of course," I say with a smile. And another sip. Wow, this wine is going to my head quickly. Warmth runs through my veins and I lean forward, elbows the counter as she continues.

"I'm a private person, you know that. I won't ask you, or Todd, anything because it's your story to tell. But, I'm here. For you and for him."

"Ag—"

Clapping her hands, she smiles broadly. "Nope. That's it. Think on it and we can talk later. Now, this show," she says, waving her arm toward the television, "a musical?"

Shrugging, I walk toward the couch and flop down on the cushions, careful not to spill my wine. "Your bestie has moved on from attempting to master languages and onto his musical range. Just a head's up, do not write a rockstar romance, he'll try to sing in the audiobook."

Snorting out a laugh, Aggi joins me on the couch. Kicking off her shoes, she pulls her feet onto the cushions and smiles. "Oh dear. I can't believe that was even remotely fun to listen to."

For the next hour, I tell Aggi about all the places Todd took me to. I couldn't stop gushing about the food at the diner or the cute shops in town. She nodded and laughed along with me.

"So you met Marcy then?"

"I did," I say, taking her empty wine glass along with mine. Placing the empty glasses in the sink, I grab two water bottles from the refrigerator. Returning to the couch, I resume my spot as she continues.

"Marcy is a sweetheart. A little awkward, which

I should not ever say about another person because we've both met me. Anyway, at first, I thought she had a major crush on Todd because she would always ask about him anytime I would see her. Then, one day I saw him in this dreadful shirt. Dancing watermelons I think," she says with her brows quirked and nose scrunched. "I don't remember, there have been so many. I'm getting off track. So, like I was saying, he was wearing this shirt and once I stopped laughing at the ridiculousness, I asked him what fashion statement he was making."

"What did he say?"

A huge smile overtakes Aggi's face and she sits up straighter, excitement evident on her face. "He told me Marcy made the shirt. Can you believe that? Not just that shirt either. Since then, almost all of the random shirts he's worn have been made by Marcy."

"Why does he wear them? Does he feel sorry for her or something?"

"What? Oh no! He wears them because he believes in supporting anyone following their dreams. Or anyone down on their luck. Or anything uninspired. Really, Todd just loves helping people. Marcy isn't the most confident person we know, but she has a talent for sewing and he has tried encouraging her to start an online shop. She doesn't think anyone would buy her shirts. To prove her wrong, Todd has been buying one a week—and wearing it, by the way—for close to two years."

My heart soars. Not flutters or twinges. No skipping a beat with affection. It soars to the highest of heights. Who does that? Who sees something in someone and then encourages and supports that person to follow their dream? Todd Chimolski. Tears prickle at the back of my eyes. Overcome with emotion over a man who I basically just shunned and didn't acknowledge, I blink rapidly, pushing the tears aside.

"Has he always been like that?" I ask, schooling my features and speaking slowly so my emotional turmoil isn't evident.

"Oh yeah. Todd's the best. He only hires local whenever possible, supports small businesses, and if there's something to be bought he's the first in line. If he had a freezer, it'd be jam-packed with cookie dough, pies, jerky, and Girl Scout cookies. Basically, any fundraising effort."

Looking at her disappointed, I say, "Sorry, girl. No cookies here. I was just in the freezer this morning."

"Oh, he doesn't live here. He lives with Bill. Well, not *with* Bill but at the building."

I open my mouth to question what she's talking about when her phone rings. Holding her finger up to keep me from speaking, she answers the call. "You've been gone like an hour. Miss us already?"

Todd.

"Oh, I don't know. Let me look." I watch as she rises from the couch and walks down the hall. She's only gone a minute when she returns with a phone charger in one hand and her cell phone in the other.

"Feel like a little road trip? He forgot his charger."

"Sure. But, doesn't he have more than one?"

Aggi breaks out in a fit of giggles. Wiping her eyes she says, "Oh Donna, Todd is the biggest tightwad I know. He doesn't drive that stupid car for nothing. He would never have two chargers. Also, it'll be fun. I can show you a few of the other highlights our area has to offer. The resort is beautiful this time of year."

She's rattling off a list of places we will drive by and some sports bar she promises me will have the best pizza I've ever had, all while I put on my snow boots. Following her out the door, I'm grateful to see she's used the remote start on her small SUV. My ass is already freezing, and I've only been out of the warm house for thirty seconds.

"This is where Todd lives?" I ask incredulously as I look out the window and up at an older building. It's not the slums or anything but it is also a far cry from the beautiful chalet-like cabin we left an hour ago.

"For now. He insists on keeping his costs down so whenever possible, he stays in one of the apartments during the construction. Actually, both he and Bill live here this time."

"You've mentioned Bill before, who is that?"

Unlatching her seat belt, she taps out a message on her phone, assumingly to Todd, then says, "His building manager? I think that's what Todd calls him. He's a former Marine and was a resident here before Todd purchased the building. He's a nice guy, but I think he had some sort of traumatic brain injury in his last deployment which makes it hard for him to work. Anyway, most of the tenants were able to find somewhere else to live during construction but Bill had nowhere to go. He'd have been homeless. So, Todd offered him not only a job but to stay living here. Basically, he keeps an eye on the property to prevent squatters. Plus, I think Todd likes that someone else is interested in learning that ridiculous bird language with him."

Soaring. That's the only way to describe what my heart is doing right now.

When Aggi's phone lights up again, she excuses herself and scurries from the car. I sit and watch as she enters through the main door to the building. Realizing I haven't checked my email all day, I open the icon on my phone and scroll until I see one from my agent.

Excitement and nerves overwhelm me. This is it. If my agent was able to sell my small town romance series, I will finally be able to write what is in my heart. Or, if he wasn't then back to dirty talking billionaires and their desire to spank asses. Taking a deep breath, I say a little wish to anyone that will listen.

Clicking the icon, my soaring heart plummets. Crash and burn. No love here.

Denied.

Want more of what you've been doing.

Sex sells.

Small town and slow burn don't sell books.

Tossing my phone in my purse, I lean my head back on the head rest and wallow in my feelings. Rejection stings, even when you're almost expecting it. My mistake was letting myself get sucked into the happy vortex Todd created. He showed me what a small town was like. What kindness and simple gestures mean to people. How easily it would be to fall into a life of simplicity with someone who is kind and affectionate. He believed in what I dreamed of doing.

If I called him right now, he'd tell me to write from the heart. Heck, he's only a few feet away with Aggi. I can just as easily jump out of this car and make my way to his door. He'd talk to me. Listen to me and tell me what to do.

He'd also tell me I already know what to do and I don't need permission to write what I feel. And, he would be right.

A cold blast of air hits me in the face as Aggi climbs back behind the wheel and slams the door. "Are you hun—" she begins but stops when she sees me. "Donna, what's wrong?"

"My agent doesn't think he can sell the book I was writing. I'll have to scrap it for something else. Something *sexier.*"

"Why do you have to scrap it?"

Sighing, I rotate my head in her direction. "My agent can't sell it."

"What's the problem? Just self-pub this book and then crank out one of your tie-'em-up-and-bang-'em books". Easy peasy."

I don't respond. Instead I ponder her words and what I know in my heart I want to do. When she pulls into a parking lot that houses a large green building, I sit up in my seat. "Ags?"

"Yeah?" She turns the car off and unclips her seatbelt before turning to face me. "What's up?"

"Do you think I could stay at the cabin a few more days? Long enough to finish this book?"

Smiling, she starts jumping in her seat. I'll take that as a yes.

"Of course! I have to leave in two days for Spencer's MRI but of course you can stay."

"Shouldn't we ask Todd? I mean, it is his house."

"Eh, it's fine. I'll shoot him a text. Now, are you ready for the best pizza of your life?"

The defeat I felt a few minutes ago dissolves and my stomach lets out a loud rumble in answer to her question. Giggling, we exit the car and make our way to the front door of the building. A week. I can finish this book in a week and still make any deadline the publisher sets for the erotica series.

As Aggi would say, easy peasy.

Chapter 20

Todd

Putting my car in park, I look up at my chalet.

And then I immediately smack my own forehead for referring to my cabin as a chalet. What has gotten into me?

Donna. That's what's gotten into me. It's been two days since "the brush off episode" as I am now referring to it, and I still can't get every part of me on board with letting it all go. My mind keeps drudging up memories everywhere. Like when I had breakfast at the diner today. Lisa kept asking about the "blonde beauty" I had with me, like any of us expected Donna to stay forever. No one stays here forever so it would be ridiculous to think otherwise just because I had breakfast with her. Right?

Sighing, I roll my eyes at myself and climb out of my car. I don't have time to have an existential crisis. I have things to do and people to hire. In particular, a new cleaning lady, the reason I'm back here in the first place. Someone has to wash the sheets and clean the kitchen before the next renter comes in. Who knows when a Kardashian might decide to stop here for a while. It's happened before. Remote resort towns are a favorite among A-listers. Yet another reason why real estate is such a good investment around here.

I step inside and shut the door behind me only to realize I'm not alone. I don't hear any loud noises, just the vibrations of another person being in the same house. Almost like a sixth sense. Bruce Willis and I have that and our sexy voices in common. Well except the part where his character didn't have a sixth sense.

Slowly, I make my way through the entry and into the living area, being as quiet as possible. I don't want to tip off the person who may be about to murder me of my presence. I may not be buff but I'm scrappy and I will take every advantage I can get, especially the element of surprise.

Rounding the corner, I see a familiar mop of blonde hair on the other side of the couch. Is she the first victim?

"Donna?" I whisper so as not to tip off the man in the mask who will inevitably attack at any moment.

"Ohmygod!" she screams as she jumps up and into her karate stance.

Throwing my own hand over my heart, I jump back. "Cheese and Crackers! What did you do to your face?!"

Her whole body relaxes as she processes my identity. Then the realization of what I'm talking about hits her. She slowly raises her finger tips to her face, scrunching her nose. The movement sends little cracks across her face.

"It's a charcoal mask. Wait, did you say *cheese and crackers*?"

Shaking my head to wave off her question, I pose my own. "You rubbed the shit from under the fire on your face?"

She attempts an exaggerated eyeroll, but since her face can't seem to move, it only partially works. "No, Todd. It's a deep cleaning face mask. Sucks all the impurities out of my pores and all that." Her words are a little mumbled as she speaks through a frozen mouth.

"It looks like you were cleaning out my chimney."

She crosses her arms and tries to raise an eyebrow. All it does is make a crack on her forehead. "If you expect me to start singing some of the tunes from Mary Poppins, you're going to be disappointed."

"If you can't belt out some Chim Chiminee, you're not the woman I thought you were."

She smirks and takes a seat on the couch, I assume because there is no threat of murder anymore. As she resituates her bathrobe around her, I make a mental note to ask her thoughts on the fluffiness later. I have a lead on another brand if they need to be replaced.

"What are you doing here anyway?" she asks.

"I was going to ask you the same thing."

"I'm staying an extra few days to get this manuscript done." Noticing the confusion on my face, she adds, "Did Aggi forget to text you?"

Pulling out my phone, I scroll through my messages. "Nope. Nothing from our good friend Agnes who left on a jet plane and doesn't know when she'll be back again." Donna looks at me blankly. "John Denver?" Still blank. "No?" She shakes her head slightly. "So disappointing. Anyway, it's no big deal. I don't have any more renters coming in until next week so you're good. I was just going to get a head start on cleaning it up. But that can wait. I'll come back when you're gone. Do you need anything while I'm here?"

She bites her lip and shakes her head in response.

"Okay," I say with a nod and begin turning toward the door. "Well then, I'll just get out of your hair—"

"Wait!"

"Yeah?"

"About the other day—"

Aaaand here we go. I was hoping to avoid the issue, but nope. We're doing it. Putting it all out there. So much for ignoring the elephant in the room.

"Todd, I'm really sorry—"

"Aw man! Don't give me that look," I interrupt, running a hand down my face.

She furrows her brow, creating more cracks on her face. "I'm not giving you a look."

"You absolutely gave me a look."

"No, I didn't." She crosses her arms, clearly getting agitated. Too bad she has no idea how long I can go at this. I have been out-arguing people for years.

"Uh, yes you did."

"I don't give looks."

Looking around the room, I ask, "Where's a mirror. Do you have a mirror?"

Cue the obligatory eyeroll. "I don't need a mirror—"

"Fine. I'll just take a picture." Pulling out my phone, I set up the camera and shove it in her face. "Say it again."

"Todd, quit." She tries to push my hands out of the way. "I'm not saying it again."

"Just do it, Donna. Make the face again."

She huffs. "Fine, I'll say it again but only because you're annoying me. Todd, I'm really sorry—"

Click.

"See?" I say turning the camera around. "The face."

"I don't make a—" And then she looks at the picture. "Ohmygod, I'm totally making a face!"

Gesturing as if to say, "I told you so," I put my phone back in my pocket.

Donna, however, looks a bit shell-shocked. "I feel like there are some people I need to find on social media and apologize for making the face at them."

Waving her off, I plop down on the couch next to her. "I'm sure most of them don't even remember." Popping my feet up on the coffee table I make myself comfortable. "Whatcha doin' anyway?"

She blows her bangs off her face. "To be honest, freaking out."

And now she has my attention.

"Because of the face?"

Smacking me lightly she starts laughing. "No. Things are not shaping up the way I expected them to, and I'm trying to sort a bunch of work stuff out."

"Like what?"

"You really want to hear about all my work problems?"

This time I quirk my own eyebrow. "You know I've been listening to Aggi babble about plot twists and character development and edits for years, right?"

"Hmm. Good point." She leans into the couch, resting her head on her fist. "I'm just frustrated. My agent turned down the sweet romance I was working on, so I have to go back to my signature erotica first—"

"Wait, wait, wait." I hold my hand up to stop her. "What do you mean your agent turned it down? What was wrong with it?"

She shrugs. "Nothing per se. My publisher doesn't want it. Says my brand is all about the sex appeal."

"Ridiculous."

"Maybe. But true. The more I thought about it, the more I realized they're right. I've built a particular brand and the guaranteed money will come from that. I see their point. I'm disappointed, but I understand from a financial perspective why they turned it down."

As much as I hate to admit it, she's right. Business isn't personal, it's all about the moola. "So what are you going to do?"

"I already had a thirty-thousand-word outline in the can so I'm finalizing that."

"Thirty thousand words?" I'm stunned. That's like a short book. And she has it as an *outline*.

"What can I say? Sometimes when I'm in the middle of one project another one tries to take over my creativity. If I do a really detailed outline, it quiets that voice, so I can finish what I'm doing and get back to it later."

I nod in appreciation because that's impressive.

"So anyway," she continues, "I'm going whip this one out since I have contractual obligations and then finish the story I want. I'll self-publish it."

"Sounds like a solid plan."

"Yeah. Well. That's only one of many problems. I also have a book releasing in three months and my narrator just cancelled at the last minute. Something about polyps on his voice box or something."

Clearing my throat, I nod my head in understanding. It's a sympathetic response to the polyps reference. Kind of like when you see another man hit in the crown jewels and can't help but double over in solidarity. "Nodes."

"What?" Her confusion shouldn't surprise me. Actually it kind of does. Pitch Perfect is a classic.

"Never mind, continue."

Looking at me like I've lost my mind she shakes her head before speaking. "We're scrambling to get someone on board quickly, but it isn't looking promising. If we don't find someone immediately and they don't start by next week, there's no way production will have it done in time for release day."

This is one of those moments in time where I have a choice to make. I can be a good friend, despite our previous fall out, and let her continue to vent. Or I can go above and beyond for someone who has a need. For me, it's a no-brainer. Although I can barely believe the words myself when they pop out of my mouth.

"I'll do it."

She pauses mid-sentence and just stares at me.

Leaning in, I give her a second, but she still doesn't respond. Or maybe she can't. That face mask is looking pretty dry and cracked. "Did you hear me or are you having some kind of a seizure? What's happening here, Donna?"

"I just—" She stops to clear her throat. "But you don't narrate for anyone except Aggi."

"No, I don't narrate for anyone except my friends."

Her eyes widen, but this time she looks delighted. Or her eyes do, at least. "Really?"

"Really. But don't go telling people or spilling the beans about my secret identity. I have enough ladies following me around. I don't need all Hawk Weaver's fans coming after me too."

She laughs and leans over, throwing her arms around me. "Thank you, Todd! Thank you! You single-handedly solved one of my work problems in a huge, huge way."

"Don't get all excited now," I say, holding her a bit tighter. I will probably regret being this close to her later, but right now I'm enjoying the feel of her again. "I hear Hawk Weaver is a real dick to work with."

Her laughter is music to my ears. So much so that I don't care she's getting that charcoal shit all over me. Maybe a little exfoliant will bring out my eyes.

Chapter 21

Donna

Three days after Todd scared the life out of me, and the same day I vowed to always lock doors when I'm indulging in a little at-home spa time, I'm zipping my suitcase with a huge smile on my face. I did it. I started and completed writing a book in a week. Okay, well, I finished the first draft of the book and have another few days of intense edits and a bunch of work behind the scenes, but I completed the story.

A sweet love story that makes my heart flutter and my palms sweat with excitement sits in my Cloud, and I feel amazing. Well, that isn't exactly true. I feel exhausted and I kind of miss my bed. And my cat. Mr. Tuddles has been the only man I could rely on the last few years, and I'm in need of a cuddle.

The only man until Todd, that is. Gosh, he certainly came out of nowhere. With his weird shirts, which I now know are worn because of his massive, genuine heart, to his weird bird language because you never know when you'll need to communicate with someone by whistling, he has found a place in my thoughts non-stop. I hate that so many miles will separate us. I've become accustomed to his presence. I don't make friends easily, but with him it was seamless.

I pick up my cell phone to confirm the status of my car and smile at the memory of him hanging out with me yesterday. While I sat nestled on the couch before another one of his roaring fires, typing away furiously on my laptop, Todd was decked out in a yellow shirt adorned with dancing flamingos as he channeled his inner nineties boyband and cleaned the cabin. Chalet. I finally have him calling this place a chalet instead of cabin, and I take a lot of satisfaction in that. I also take a lot of satisfaction in watching his tight little booty shake when he was dusting. That's a visual image I'll have with me for a while.

With only a few minutes before the car arrives, I pull the suitcase from the bed and drag it down the hall to the foyer. I had hoped Todd would swing by to say goodbye, but he already had a commitment for work. The real estate mogul work, not the new narration gig for the super talented, and if I may, quite pretty, erotica romance author. That author would be me, of course.

I take one last look around the cabin and just as I hear the telltale sound of a car pulling up on the wet driveway, I rush to the kitchen to double check the stove knobs. I didn't use them the last few days, but it's an irrational fear I have, so I confirm they are turned off before returning to the foyer. Once I'm outside and settled into the car, I lay my head on the head rest and tilt it to look out the window. The beauty of this place will sit in my memories for a lifetime. The snow-capped trees remind me of a postcard and I quickly pull my phone from my purse and snap a photo to upload onto my social media.

Inspiration comes in many forms, and I'm happy to say being in this sleepy little town nestled in the mountains of Idaho, I found mine. Of course, the sweet man who played tour guide didn't hurt. I let the memories embrace me as we drive to the airport.

Although everywhere I look as we drive along the interstate is covered in miles and miles of snow, the roads are clear, and our drive is quick and painless. I've found another bonus to this part of the country—no traffic. At least not the kind of traffic I'm used to.

I'm also not used to how few people are at the airport. My trek through security is quicker than I anticipated and with two hours to spare before my flight, I have the luxury of heading straight for the small bar near my gate to get some work done. Once I've powered up my laptop and ordered a glass of wine and a salad, I open my manuscript to begin the traitorous task of self-editing. But before I'm able to read a complete sentence, my phone rings.

"Yes, I'm at the airport. No, I am not running late," I say to Clara as I whisper a "thank you" to the server when she sets my wine glass in front of me.

"Why would you leave that glorious place? It's magnificent."

"It is. But how do you know that? I only sent you one picture and that was of the beautiful bathroom at the cabin. I mean chalet. Never mind."

Clara is quiet for a minute, the sounds of a door closing and her keys clanking in the background. If I were guessing, I'd assume she just walked in her apartment and tossed her keys in the nearby large bowl she painted at one of those paint and bake places.

"I am your best friend. Clearly, I stalk all your social media. Which, by the way, has been dead the entire time you've been gone. I'm sure your *people* are pissed about that." Clara's always teasing me about my team, calling them my *people* like I have an entourage.

In the beginning, it would frustrate me because I would never call the team that supports me anything other than my biggest supporters. Now I know she does it to tease me because she knows how hard we all work and the common goal is simple. Build a kick-ass business so I can take her on an all-expenses-paid trip to the tropics.

Every year.

"I sent a message to my assistant when we were in town one day to let her know the reception was minimal, but I was working. You should be grateful I didn't post much. The level of your jealousy would have been off the charts."

"Yeah, yeah. Stop rubbing it in. I know you had a *working vacation* while I was stuck here with your cat."

Sipping my wine, I sit smugly while she regales me with all that I've missed in Phoenix. Which, by the way, isn't much.

As she's telling me about Mr. Tuddles and his

recent adventures with a new toy she bought him, a handsome man in a suit sits at the table next to me. Instead of sitting so we're side by side, he takes the seat that faces me. The tables in this small bar are so close together, he might as well have taken the seat at my table.

Smiling at the man as Clara finishes her story, I ask her a very important question. "What's the weather there right now? I know it's Phoenix but is it early winter temps or late winter temps?"

The server drops off my salad and I mouth another "thank you" as Clara reminds me there isn't too much of a difference, but it is in fact warmer than usual. Sighing, I comment, "I'm probably going to melt. I think I've acclimated to actual winter since I've been here."

"Well, don't sweat all over my car when I pick you up. Oh, we're meeting the girls tonight at eight for cocktails. See you when you land!" The call disconnects before I can respond.

Closing my laptop, I rearrange my table so I can enjoy my salad. I no sooner stuff a huge bite in my mouth than the handsome suit next to me says, "Sorry, I couldn't help overhearing. Are you headed to Phoenix?"

Coughing as I try to quickly chew and swallow the food in my mouth, I bring my napkin to my mouth and nod.

"Sorry, bad timing. Are you okay? Can I get you a water?"

Waving off the stranger's offer, I finish the process

and take a sip of my wine before turning my attention to him. "I'm okay. Sorry. Umm, yes, I am. I live there. How about you?"

There's probably some written rule about sharing personal information with a stranger you meet in an airport bar, but considering I almost died by romaine lettuce, I think I'm safe.

"I'm heading there for business. Did your husband confirm the weather? I realized I didn't exactly pack for warmer weather and may need to do some quick shopping while I'm there."

Oh he's slick. Throwing out the husband card to see if I'm single. I've written that into a book a time or two. It works every single time. And, I'll admit, the way he fills out a suit and wears a watch, it might be working in real life. Don't question the watch, a beautiful watch on a man's wrist is sexy.

"I'm Donna," I say instead of responding to his query.

"Donna, it's a pleasure. Joe Corman." Joe's hand clasps mine. The grip is strong but not too strong. His hands are soft, and his cologne is pleasant. His dark hair has that look I seek out for my book covers, slightly mussed but still perfectly in place. This man knows his fashion. From his perfectly tailored suit to the pricey cufflinks, he oozes successful business man. He's everything I would have asked for on my online dating profile. Everything I would write into a book. If he were a book, his cover would be selling a lot of copies.

While standing, Joe removes his suit coat and slings it across the empty seat at his table before resuming his spot. The server delivers his bottle of beer, and over drinks and a half-eaten salad, we spend the rest of the time before our flight talking and laughing. His arrogance isn't over the top but enough that I'd call him just teetering on the alpha side of things.

When we board the plane, Joe asks to switch seats with the person in the middle of my row so that we can continue our conversation. I'm not complaining. It's easy to talk to Joe. Not as easy and fun as Todd, but easy nonetheless. He works in the insurance industry and is headed to Phoenix for some sort of speaking engagement. What is it with this part of the country? Does everyone who wears a suit speak to large groups of people?

We spend the entirety of the flight laughing and enjoying each other's company. That's way more than I can say for the flight to Idaho. Maybe, just maybe the fates are finally aligning.

"Ladies and gentlemen, as we make our descent into Phoenix, we wanted to express our gratitude for flying with us. Your flight crew will be coming through the cabin to gather any items you may wish to discard. Buckle up, and we'll be on the ground shortly."

Pulling my trash from the seat pocket in front of me, I am startled when Joe's hand rests on my arm. "Donna, I've really enjoyed spending time with you. In many ways, it felt a little like a first date. Only, I didn't get your number or buy you a drink. I think we should rectify both of those. What do you say?"

Double blinking my eyes, I ponder his suggestion. My first instinct is to say no. I don't want to go out on a date with a stranger. But, he's right. We've spent the last few hours together getting to know one another, not unlike a first date. Plus, he's nice and funny and successful. He's everything I've ever looked for in a man. I don't want to miss out on an opportunity to get to know him better, do I? No. No, I don't. So, without another thought, I say, "Sounds great."

I can't wait to tell Clara that her assessment of putting out into the world what I want may be partly true. I just finished writing a book about an alpha male who is more than he seems and I just found one on the plane.

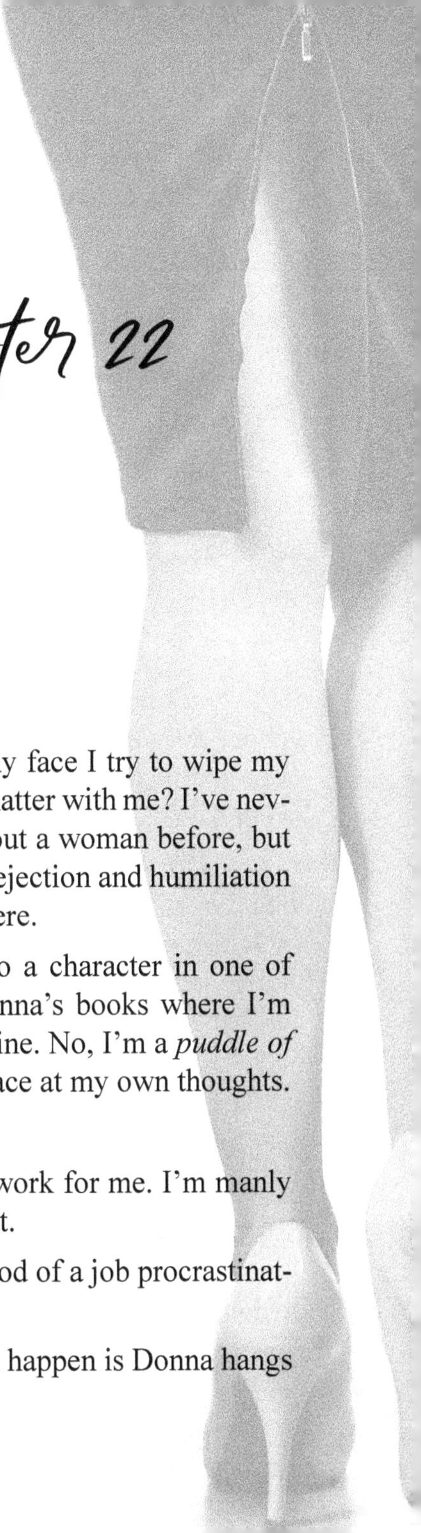

Chapter 22

Todd

I should call her.

Maybe.

I'm not sure.

Rubbing my hand down my face I try to wipe my frustration away. What is the matter with me? I've never been so tied up in knots about a woman before, but Donna has me worried about rejection and humiliation and putting my feelings out there.

Ohmygod. I've turned into a character in one of Aggi's books. Not one of Donna's books where I'm strong and broody and masculine. No, I'm a *puddle of emotions* and *sensitive*. I grimace at my own thoughts.

Holy shit, I'm Spencer.

Nope. This isn't going to work for me. I'm manly and alpha or some shit like that.

And I'm doing way too good of a job procrastinating this phone call.

Fuck it. The worst that can happen is Donna hangs

up on me, posts my picture on social media with Hawk Weaver's name under it, and tells everyone what a bad kisser I am.

I think for a minute and then shrug. "Sounds like my high school experience. I'll be fine."

Before I lose my nerve, I dial her number and wait for her to pick up.

It rings. And rings. And rings.

As I'm preparing to leave a voicemail, she finally answers.

"Hello?" She sounds out of breath.

"Uh," I pause. "Did I call at a bad time?"

"No!" she practically yells, forcing me to pull the phone away from my ear. "Sorry. That was loud. No. I was getting out of the shower, and I didn't want to miss your call."

This is the part where my brain shorts out for a number of reasons. First, she just got out of the shower. Which means she's naked. Probably with a white fluffy towel wrapped around her body, blonde hair piled high on her head as water droplets slide down her golden tan skin.

To be honest, it's more likely she still has soap in her hair and mascara dripping down her face, legs half shaved. Still naked. In a towel.

Either way, these are not visual images I need to be having right now. Both options are desirable, and it would be rude for me to get a hard-on while having this conversation. Yet, there it is. Inappropriately stiff and wishing I could ask which version of her is happening right now. The naked one or . . . well, the naked one.

That's not the only reason I have to get my bearings straight again. Donna just said she didn't want to miss my call. Because of business or Aggi or because she misses me? The possibilities are endless!

See? *Emotional puddle*. Just take my mancard away. I have no use for it any more. Spencer and I might as well have a sleepover and braid each other's hair.

"Todd? Are you there?"

Breaking out of my deep thoughts, not with Jack Handy, I realize I must have been visualizing this scenario longer than I thought.

"Yeah." I clear my throat and try again. "Yeah. Sorry. I got sidetracked."

By thoughts of you in the shower . . .

"Do I need to call you back?"

"No! No. Give me just a second, will you?"

I listen as she puts the phone down and hear sounds of drawers opening and closing, her pulling panties up her legs, sliding a bra over her arms . . .

Okay, my thoughts are spiraling. Quick, Todd. Think about cleaning toilets and the last time Mom's cat jumped on my leg and slid down, shredding my pants.

"Okay, I'm back." She sounds breathy like she's been exerting herself, and it's doing nothing to get my thoughts back on track. All I can think about is how certain parts of her body are probably jiggling. "So, how are you?"

Such a loaded question . . .

"Good. I'm doing good, thanks. I uh, actually called because I have news."

"Okay."

"I'll email you the sample today, but I sent the book over to production, so they'll start editing in the next couple of days."

"Wait, wait, wait," she says rapidly. It's not hard to hear the disbelief in her voice. "You're already done narrating my book?"

"Yeppers."

"How is that possible?"

"Uh . . . I sat down at my work station and did it? I don't understand the question."

She giggles lightly. "Todd, you've had my manuscript for like three days. How is that possible?"

"It's been closer to five days, and you forget how flexible my boss is."

"I'll say. Let him know I owe him one."

And now for more dirty thoughts. *Don't go there, Todd.*

"I can't wait to hear the sample, though," she continues, and I focus on business. That's what we're talking about. Job . . . stuff. "You wouldn't want to, uh, read it to me so I can get a feel for it, would you?"

My eyebrows shoot up. That's not a request I was

expecting.

"I know that sounds weird," she continues, talking faster than normal so I know she's nervous to even ask. It makes me smile. "I've been so stressed about this deadline, and I wasn't anticipating you'd get it done so fast. Hearing a part of it will go a long way to calm my nerves about the whole situation."

Still an odd request, but I'm not an author. I guess it's not much different than when I want to double check a contract before one of my team members goes to closing. We all have a bit of micromanaging in us where our businesses are concerned.

"Uh yeah. Sure. I just need to head to my studio to grab the book."

"You have a real studio?"

No.

"Sure I do! Just don't ask Aggi about it. You know how she likes to lie about these things and say it's just a closet."

"Todd, is it just a closet?"

"Donna. Just because I store my clothes in my studio doesn't make it a closet."

Donna laughs as I open my closet door and push the suits farther back on the rack before sitting down. I set up my tablet and scroll until I find the file with all my notes on it. The system basically lets me turn the book into a script so I know where to use inflection or maybe a fancy British accent. Not that Donna or Aggi has ever given me the opportunity to show off that skill. *Yet*.

"How's it feel to be back in Phoenix, anyway?" I ask while I wait for everything to open.

"Hot. I honestly thought I was going to have a heat stroke as soon as I walked out of the airport."

"I seem to remember a very debonair fella suggesting you were dressed too warm."

"Hey!" she chuckles. "I'm not a cold weather gal. I needed that fluffy coat."

"And now you will never wear it again." Glancing at the script as it loads, I make sure it's the final version. Satisfied that I've found the right document, I exclaim, "Okay! Got it. I'm gonna put you on speaker for this."

"Which part are you reading?" she asks, half in my ear, half in the room as I put my phone on speaker as I set it on the desk. Her voice fills the room.

I shrug even though she can't see it. "No idea. Whatever pulls up for me. We'll consider it a surprise. You ready?"

"Hang on. I need to get comfortable." I listen as she shifts around, envisioning her lying in her bed wearing just a small tank top and short shorts, hair fanned out on her pillow with come-hither eyes looking up at me.

Focus, Todd!

"Okay. I'm ready."

"Yeah, you are," I mutter to myself.

"What?"

"Nothing. This might be rough at first since I don't know where I'm starting so remember it'll be better in the sample."

"I'm not worried about it."

Clearing my throat, I lower my voice an octave to bring forth Hawk Weaver and begin reading.

"Lie down on the bed, I instruct. She complies like a good girl and my eyes are glued to her naked ass as she crawls to the headboard, supple and ready for the taking. Her pussy glistens with her arousal, making my dick hard as a rock."

"Todd," Donna says softly. "You're really starting with that scene?"

"Uh . . . yeah. It appears that I am. Does that make you uncomfortable?"

She takes a beat before answering. "No. I mean, they're my words and I'm going to hear you read them eventually anyway. Go ahead. Keep going."

I clear my throat again, partially to get into character. Partially because this conversation has gone in a completely different direction than I anticipated when I first dialed her number. I expected interesting conversation, but not *this* kind of interesting. Not that I'm not enjoying myself. Just ask the man in my pants.

Down boy.

"Stay on your knees, I growl, and she stops, shifting her body so her heavy tits touch the bed and her ass raises up another inch. The sound of my hand smacking her ass makes a loud thwack. She gasps—"

Donna gasps too, and I momentarily stumble over my words.

"and, um . . . and I immediately caress the sting out of red mark left behind by my hand. So beautiful, I whisper and lower myself to kiss the same spot I'm caressing. Her skin tastes like salt and musk, and in an instant my lips are on her core, licking up her slit. She groans—"

Donna groans as well, and now it's taking everything in me not to whip my dick out of my pants and keep talking dirty to her until we both finish this. I hear her shifting, the rustling of her bedding in the background. Visions of her touching herself as she moves sends another jolt of desire through me. I'm not sure what is actually happening on her end or how my calling to give her an update on this project has turned into me reading her a sex scene and possibly having phone sex.

Are we even having phone sex? Or am I misinterpreting all her noises? Is she just getting into the story? Doesn't matter. I can't stop now. I have to keep reading.

"and pushes her body back, grinding her swollen pussy into my face as I thrust my tongue in and out of her. My fingers dig into her hips and I nip and suck, faster, deeper—"

"Ohmygod—"

"until I decide I've had enough. I'm the one running this show. She's not the only one who will get pleasure tonight. Grabbing a condom off the bedside table, I make quick work of rolling it down my length and within in seconds I'm plunging inside her, my balls slapping hard against her clit—"

I barely register the sound of a cough coming from above me as I read until Donna finally stops me.

"Uh . . . Todd?"

"Hold on, I'm getting to the good part. *Gripping her hips I slam into her harder—*"

"No seriously, Todd, who is coughing in the background?"

Suddenly, I register exactly what she's talking about. It's Bill having some sort of massive bronchial attack. I'm slightly frustrated by the interruption, but more worried about why he's coughing up a lung. I don't need blood on those floors. The hardwood was stained yesterday.

"Cover your ear, Donna," I instruct, then let out a shrill whistle followed by calling out to Bill. "You okay up there? Do I need to call the coroner?"

An irritated whistle calls back to me.

"Yeah, fuck you too, buddy," I say in response to his cussing me out in bird language. How rude. "Sorry about that, Donna. Shall I continue? It sounds like you were enjoying yourself."

"Um . . . about that . . ."

And here we go. Regret and the ever cliché "I was caught up in the moment" response.

"If I can hear Bill, does that mean he can hear me?"

"No."

"Tooooddddd?"

Maybe. I honestly don't know.

"Relax, Donna. Let's test it out okay? I'm sure it's fine. Bill, can you hear me?" I ask at normal volume, like I'm having a conversation with the person sitting next to me.

The low whistle back comes as a completely surprise.

"Huh. I had no idea. This is going to put a kink in my porn watching time, isn't it?"

Bill whistles yet another reply.

"I wasn't talking to you, Bill!" I yell and bang on the ceiling with the broomstick I use for times like these. Then shaking my head I pick up the phone and take it off speaker. "You still there?"

"Surprisingly, I have not hung up yet, despite my mortification about what just happened and how there was a witness."

"Eh. It's just Bill. Who's he gonna tell?"

"While that is a good point, my face is beet red, so I'm going to hang up so I can pretend this entire conversation never happened."

Before my mouth is open enough to respond, Donna has already disconnected the call. "Thanks a lot, Bill," I mutter, eliciting yet another inappropriate whistle of response.

"Language!" I yell, sounding irritated, and yet, I can't stop smiling. I'm not sure what just happened, but whatever rejection I felt before is gone. In its place is the thought that maybe, just maybe, Donna and I aren't over quite yet.

Chapter 23

Donna

One thousand. That's how many times I've died internally replaying my call with Todd. For the last four hours I've ignored all of his texts. And calls. If Airplane Joe had called to confirm our date for tonight, I would have answered, feigned illness, and cancelled. I'm mortified.

Not because some random man heard him reading my book. I couldn't care less about that. I don't know Bill and will probably never meet him. No, it's because of the reaction I had to Todd reading the words. The words I created and put in a book. A book that in only a few weeks will be heard by listeners across the globe. Sure, this isn't my first audiobook, but it's the first book the narrator read to me over the phone. A narrator I know.

As the words flowed across the line, my insides warmed, and my heart raced. Like it is now. Just thinking of Todd, er, Hawk, saying the word "pussy" has my suddenly overactive libido on hyperdrive. The moment he started speaking, I relaxed in a way that only seems to be possible when he's around. What are the chances that the one part of the book he randomly chose to read was one of the hottest scenes I've ever written? It's also one of the hardest scenes I've ever written. Sex is hard. Not actual sex, at least I don't remember it being hard. It's been so long, I can't be trusted to offer a true assessment.

Stupid Todd.

Stupid Todd and his so sexy voice and amazing hands and freaking adorable smirk. Dammit to hell, this is not what I should be thinking about while I get ready for a date. A date with a man who checks all of my boxes. A man who is successful, handsome, smart, and seems to have a great sense of humor.

As I swipe the mascara across my lashes, I realize those four boxes on my list are also checked by Todd. Add in the way he wears a suit, and how he encouraged me to follow my heart, and he just might have a slight edge on airplane Joe.

Focus, Donna. Joe is your date. Todd is your friend.

My phone chimes another text message, this one from Aggi.

Aggi: Are you ready for the NANA noms?

Me: Ugh. I forgot that was happening. I'm not expecting much.

Aggi: Oh hush. Your books rock. I bet you make the finals.

Me: We'll see. I have a date tonight so I'm more focused on that.

Aggi: Oh a date! I can't wait to hear about it.

Me: Chill. It's a FIRST date.

Aggi: Still. Have fun and let me know how it goes!

I don't bother responding and toss my phone on the counter while I finish my makeup. A final swipe of mascara and a bright red lip later and I'm happy enough with how I look. Truth be told, I'm missing the easiness of life at the cabin. Minimal makeup, messy bun, and sweats. Sounds heavenly right now.

Instead of my comfy sweats, I pull my usual black dress from the closet. Hesitating, I look to the right and see a blue geometric skirt I bought ages ago and have yet to wear. Maybe the black dress, the one I've worn on almost all my first dates this past year, is bad mojo. I like Joe and would like this to be a good first date. Well, I guess second if I go with his assessment from the plane. Hanging the dress back in its spot, I grab the skirt and a fitted black sweater before exiting my closet.

I'm pulling the sweater over my head when the doorbell rings. I quickly grab my black heels and hustle down the hall to answer the door. Pausing at the door to slip on my shoes and right myself, I take a deep breath and open the door.

Standing before me is a cover model. Not an actual cover model but a man who could easily grace the cover of any modern romance novel. Specifically one of my erotica romances. Hot damn.

"Wow," Joe says with an appreciative whistle. "You look amazing."

I smile at his compliment and realize I probably look completely different than his travel companion the other day. Traveling isn't exactly meant to be done in a pencil skirt and four-inch heels.

"Thank you. You're quite dapper in that suit." I step aside to let him in the apartment. "I'll just be one minute, I need to grab my purse."

Rushing down the hall, I grab my small clutch from the top of my dresser and return to the living room where I stop in my tracks. Joe is standing in the spot I left him, his back to the closed door and a look of horror on his face. Mr. Tuddles sits before him, his head cocked to the side.

"Wha . . . what is wrong with your cat?" he whispers.

"Mr. Tuddles? Nothing, why?"

"He has no hair."

"Oh, that. Yeah, it's a little weird at first but he's the best."

I can tell Mr. Tuddles' appearance is freaking Joe out so I shoo him away and tell him to go to bed so we can leave. When he turns his back on us and begins his slow retreat to the bedroom, Joe visibly relaxes. I've never seen someone react to my cat like that. Sure, he's not what most people expect when I tell them I have a cat, but he's sweet and a little awkward and overall, amazing. He loves me, like I love him.

"Shall we go?" I ask, pulling Joe from his frozen

state. Nodding, he clears his throat and steps aside before opening the door. As I step through the threshold, he places a hand to my lower back and guides me down the hall and to the elevator.

"Sorry I reacted so poorly. I was surprised and then he just sat there staring at me. I was a little unnerved." I appreciate his concern with my feelings, not that he needs to explain. It's not every day you see a hairless cat. Well, unless you're me and you live with one.

"I understand. No big deal. Where are we headed?" I ask as we exit the building and walk to the small parking lot. Lights flash on a white sedan and I follow Joe to the car. When he opens the door for me, I pause before getting in to look at him as he speaks.

"I was thinking we could try this little bistro that has a great Yelp rating. It's only about ten minutes from here."

I know exactly which one he's talking about. Great. Back to the scene of the crime of my worst date in all my dating years. Fingers crossed Joe doesn't have a carrot cake eating wife too.

Since Joe and I spent so many hours talking on our flight, tonight doesn't hold the same level of awkwardness of most first dates. He regales me with a basic rundown of his day and I do the same. We order our food and enjoy a glass of wine while we discuss the important things in life: How did Lois Lane not know Clark was Superman? Why don't we have to refrigerate peanut butter after it's opened?

Joe refills each of our wine glasses before he asks the question I dreaded. "So how is it you found yourself writing romance books?" I'm never quite certain how to answer this question. I could offer him a generic "I just fell into it" response or I could be honest. I was heartbroken, drunk, and horny when an idea came to me. I decide on a combination of both.

"It's a pretty boring story. I was working for a large firm downtown, busting my ass to stand out among the other associates. After one very long day of dealing with irate clients, a jammed copier, and a broken heel on my favorite pair of shoes, I went home to have my boyfriend use the it's-not-you,-it's-me line. Half a bottle of tequila later, I had an outline and the first few chapters of my first novel."

"That's impressive. And your ex sounds like a jerk, but I have no doubt it was all him."

Smiling, I take a sip of my wine and continue. "Thank you for saying that but I think it actually *was* me." Laughing, I realize that's completely true. For the first time, I acknowledge that the life I was living then didn't make me happy. I wasn't fulfilled in my career choice and truthfully, I wasn't happy in my relationship. I was phoning it all in.

"I worked a lot and when I was home, I complained about work. In the end, it all worked out. He moved out, met someone else, and they're blissfully married with like four kids or something. And, I'm living my best life. I work for myself, and I have amazing friends and a career that challenges me every day."

"Wow, you make it sound amazing. Good for you. Not everyone would take the risk you did. I commend you."

Joe and I continue with our dinner and the conversation continues to flow. He's kind and attentive, asking all the right questions and responding positively and with just the right amount of flirting to cause me to blush on occasion.

There's just one issue.

He's trying too hard. Or maybe I'm not receiving it well enough. I'm not sure. It all just feels off. Out of balance. There's no natural flow to our banter. It's more like a professional conversation, not like two people with shared interests and an obvious attraction to one another.

As he talks, I look across the table at him, my carrot cake sitting untouched in front of me. I wanted that cake so badly and now that I have it, I'm less impressed than I should be. It's a great cake. It's just not what I want anymore.

Like Joe. He's everything I wanted in a man. But he's not Todd.

Stupid Todd.

Chapter 24

Todd

I understand now why Donna was so cold at the cabin. Because it takes time to acclimate to real weather when you live in *Satan's armpit*.

No, seriously. I feel like I've been walking around the seventh circle of hell over the last two days as I've been touring properties in the northwest corner of Phoenix. The nice thing is, it's a dry heat so I don't feel like I'm breathing in soup. But that also means the second sunlight hits my skin, it feels like the top layer of my epidermis is burning. This is concerning because I prefer my epidermis where it's at and not fried off.

However, if I can't get off the phone with my mother, I'm going to be in some serious hot water anyway. All because of her damn cat.

"I just don't understand what's wrong with Ginger."

"You mean besides his stupid name?"

"Stop that, Todd," she reprimands. "Cats feel emotions too, you know. And Ginger is more sensitive because he's a rescue."

She sounds way more concerned about her devil feline than she did about me as a child. I'd be offended, but I'm too busy seeing how this conversation is going to play out.

"But ever since we got home, he acts hungry all the time. Did you feed him twice a day while we were on the cruise?"

"Uh . . . yes."

"Todd Chimoski! You didn't forget to feed Ginger did you? No wonder he's acting malnourished."

I roll my eyes because that cat could never look malnourished. He's about ten pounds too big to be called petite. "Relax, Mom. I swear on Nana's grave he did not miss a meal while you were gone."

"Your grandmother isn't dead, Todd."

"Which is why my promise is even more powerful." What I won't promise her, however, is that I cheated and got him a self-feeder so I didn't have to protect my legs from his claws twice a day for a week. If she knew, she'd come after me with her wooden spoon. Fingers crossed she doesn't go up in the garage attic where it is currently stored until the next time she goes on vacation.

She sighs heavily into the phone. "I just don't get it. It's like his entire feeding schedule is off."

Glancing around me, I realize I've reached my destination, and not a minute too soon. Sweat in my butt crack isn't comfortable at all. I honestly don't know how people live in this part of the country. And yet here I am, contemplating properties for purchase myself. Go figure.

"So get him a self-feeder, Ma."

"We talked about this Todd. Feeding shouldn't be a free-for-all. It needs to be at specific times—wait a minute."

Uh oh. I have a bad feeling this conversation is about to go south.

"Todd Chimolski! Did you get my baby a self-feeder?"

My eyes widen for half a second before I begin blowing into the receiver. "What, ma?" Another blow. "The wind kicked up. I can't hear you."

I continue to blow, making it hard, but not impossible to hear her yelling, "You cut that out right now, Todd! You ruined my cat!"

"Gottagoloveyoubye." I disconnect before she figures out there's a self-cleaning litter box in the attic too. That would get her really riled up.

Besides, I'm on a mission.

Thankfully, it wasn't hard finding the building I'm standing now in, nor was it hard to get inside and away from the threat of melting on the sidewalk.

I rap on door 7B a couple times and turn to look over the stairwell railing. The building is in good shape. Looks to be recently renovated. Fresh paint. Solid trim around all the doors and ceiling. I make a mental note to contact the property management company and see if I can get some information about local taxes and building fees.

Behind me, I hear the door open so I turn around, half excited, half nervous for this surprise visit. The surprise is on me, though.

"Jiminy Cricket, woman!" I exclaim, clutching my rapidly beating heart. "Why do you always have that shit on your face?"

Donna's caked-on face cracks as she smiles and squeals. "Todd!" Launching herself into my arms, I realize she is probably getting some of that gunk on my suit. But when she says, "I missed you," in my ear, I no longer care and hold her a little tighter.

"You did?"

"Oh course I did!" she says with a laugh, pulling back and grabbing my hand to lead me into her apartment. It's not huge, but considering she lives in a somewhat pricy area, I didn't expect a mansion. The walls of the living area are painted a soft buttercream, the same color I usually recommend to my clients, with furniture in a complementary gray. An ugly door leading to a small balcony chops up the space in a very aesthetically displeasing way. But again, pricey area of town means you don't get all the bells and whistles. And there is a good-sized open kitchen with decent dining area, so the tradeoff for an ugly door was definitely worth it.

"It's funny how used to someone you get after spending the better part of a week with them, right?" Donna continues and plops down on the couch, pulling her feet underneath her. "Have a seat. What are you doing in Phoenix? Wait. How did you get in the building?"

Contemplating my answer, I sit next to her and get comfortable like no time has passed. But it has. It's been a couple weeks since she left our home away from home and it would probably be creepy to tell her I couldn't stand it anymore, so I took the opportunity to travel to Phoenix to see her. Nope. No reason to give her a stalker vibe. Instead, I go with the secondary part of the truth.

"The security desk was empty. Not exactly comforting, Donna." She scrunches her face in the cutest possible way. Smiling in response, I continue, "I have a buddy who works down here," I say as I prop my feet up on the table. "He's been wanting to get into real estate for a while and I finally caved and came to see if it was worth helping him out."

"Is he another realtor?"

I huff through my nose. "Uh, no. He's a computer guy who wants to turn business owner but has zero skills beyond coding."

She furrows her brow, cracking more of that mask thingy. "So why does he want to do real estate?"

"No idea. But hey, if he's willing to take all the state licensing tests and front some of the start-up costs, it's at least worth looking into expanding what I'm already doing, right?"

Her smile is so big and bright right now it practically lights up the room. The room that is already bright because it's the middle of the day, but that is irrelevant. The point is it makes me happy to see it.

"If that means you'll be down here visiting regularly, I think it's the best idea your coding friend has ever had."

My eyebrows shoot up. I didn't expect she would feel that way. Sure, I was hoping. But that's as far as my rational feelings had gotten. Almost immediately, something catches my eye over her shoulder and my traitorous eyebrows furrow and fall. "Uh, Donna? What the hell is that alien sitting on the table? Tell me it's not real."

She turns to look and turns back with a smile and a giggle. "My cat? Mr. Tuddles?"

"That's not a cat. It's is a giant rat, and it's scowling at me."

She jumps up off the couch and approaches the odd-looking creature, snuggling him to her and cooing at it. "You're not a rat, are you Mr. Tuddles? You're the best kitty in the world, aren't you? Yes you are." She stands for longer than a hot second exchanging googly eyes with the hairless wonder who does, in fact, purr and meow like a feline. I'm still not convinced, though.

"He's giving me the evil eye."

"He is not." Donna laughs, dropping him on the floor gently. "He's just a bit territorial."

"Oh good. I was hoping to have a weird looking cat pee on my leg today."

Hands on her hips, Donna purses her lips. "That's not how it works. If he was going to mark his territory, he'd pee on me."

I cock my head at her, willing her to understand

why that statement is not making a better case for having an abomination as a pet.

Rolling her eyes, she ignores me and my obvious aversion to any living thing that might urinate on people for fun. "Forget Mr. Tuddles. Since you surprised me with your visit, I need to go wash this mask off and change my clothes. You hungry? We can go grab something to eat. I was going to order in, but it'll do me some good to tear my eyes away from my screen."

"Still working on that sweet romance?"

"Nope," she says, sounding way more pleased than I would expect since she just told me her passion project isn't being worked on. "That's all finished and in editing." Ah. Now it makes more sense. "I'm almost finished with the one for my agent. You know, the erotica book I had an outline for."

"You mean the one you had a small book already written for."

"Same thing. Anyway, I'll be right back. I'm getting hungry." Her hand drops on my shoulder and squeezes as she walks by.

I watch her hips sway as she walks away, relieved that I wasn't kicked out before I stepped foot inside the apartment. You never know what's going to happen when you show up at someone's house unannounced.

Tearing my eyes away from the door she just closed, presumably to her bedroom, I'm startled when I see the alien thing sitting on the coffee table in front of me, staring me down.

"What?" I ask as I cock my head, careful not to

make any sudden movements. "Do I have mustard on my tie? Something in my teeth? Bad breath?"

The faux feline responds with a strong "meeooww."

"Okay. Well, I'm not here to cause any harm, and I don't want to meet your leader, so if you could just"—I wave my hands in front of me—"shoo or something. That would be great."

He rapidly blinks at me before his eyes fixate on mine. I accept that challenge and widen my eyes in response.

"No really," I plead, refusing to blink. "Please don't pee on me. I have two more days here and don't have time to get this pee-cleaned if you decide to mark me."

Mr. Tuddles, who has probably the stupidest name I've ever heard of for a cat, which is saying a lot considering my mother named her spawn of Satan Ginger instead of Fruit of the Devil's Loins, begins walking back and forth in front of me, swishing his tail forcefully. That's right you inferior feline, I am still the reigning champion.

"Uh . . . what are you doing there . . . kitty? That's not the pee-pee dance, is it?"

A few more treks across the table and he jumps for the couch, making me startle backward a few inches and guard myself from the inevitable spray.

It never comes, though. Instead, he begins rubbing his head all over my leg. And arm. And chest. Suddenly, he's standing on my lap, meowing and still rubbing.

Well take that Fruit of the Devil's Loins. It's not me, it's you.

I begin petting Mr. Tuddles, which admittedly feels like running my hand over my last Thanksgiving dinner before it was cooked and scrumptious. But he seems to like it, as proven by the fact that he lies down and curls up on my lap.

Huh. This isn't so bad.

I keep rubbing behind his weird little ears until Donna emerges from her bedroom, dressed in white shorts that show off her tanned legs and . . . I don't know what else, actually. I'm stuck staring at her legs. When she sees us, she stops in her tracks.

"What's going on in here?" she asks, amusement thickly laced through her voice.

"Bonding. Leave us be."

"No way." With three quick steps, she's standing in front of me, pushing an unimpressed Mr. Tuddles off my lap and pulling me into standing position. "I'm hungry. You can do your weird male bonding later. Um . . ." Turning to face me, she gestures to my clothes. "We're walking. Are you sure you want to wear that?"

"As opposed to something in your closet?" I playfully chide. "Got a nice pair of yoga pants with my name on them or something?"

She smacks my arm. "No, you jerk. Why don't you leave your suit jacket here instead of wearing it? Roll up your sleeves. It'll be more comfortable."

"What would be more comfortable is if you lived in a city that didn't sit directly on the surface of the sun," I quip, making quick work of tossing my suit coat on her couch and rolling up my sleeves.

"Too late for that, ya big baby."

Looking up, she's staring at my arms, a strange look on her face. "What? What are you looking at?"

"Just thinking," she says by way of explanation.

"Wanna give me more than that?"

Looking me dead in the eye, she says the last thing I expected. "I've always heard a man is a hundred times sexier when he rolls up his shirt sleeves. I was thinking how accurate that is."

My eyebrows shoot up in surprise again. Is Donna saying she thinks I'm sexy? Me? Todd, the guy in the funny shirts who uses his closet as a studio and whistles instead of talks?

"You can stop looking so surprised and close your mouth now," she deadpans, and I snap my jaw shut.

Grabbing my wallet and phone out of the inside pockets of my jacket, I begin shoving them in my pants pockets instead, trying not to drop my phone as it vibrates. "You can't just throw something like that at me. You know how often people use the words *Todd* and *sexy* in the same sentence? Not as often as they should, that's for sure."

"Shut up," she laughs, snatching her keys from a bowl on the kitchen counter. "Let's go."

"Right behind you." But I'm not. I'm checking the text that just came through from Aggi and having no idea what the hell she's talking about. NANA? What the hell is NANA and why is it in capital letters followed by about four million exclamation points?

Donna comes up behind me, probably since I haven't moved since I said I was behind her. "Everything okay?"

"No idea. I think Aggi has officially lost her marbles."

"Wouldn't be the first time," Donna responds quietly. She's not wrong. "Why? What's going on?"

Leaning so she can see my text, I try my best to explain. "She said something about being up for a nana. Did she forget a word or something? Why is she talking about my grandmother?"

I look up and see Donna's eyes as wide as her mouth is. "You're up for a NANA?"

Now I'm really confused. "I have no idea what anyone is talking about and why they keep dragging my poor nana into our lives. She has enough troubles in the nursing home. That bitch Gretchen always changes the soap opera before it's over."

Donna thwacks me on the arm again. "Don't joke about the elderly that way." Huh. I didn't know she was such a philanthropist. "Aggi's not yelling about your nana. It's an acronym for National Association of Narrators Awards."

I shake my head slowly. "Yeah, still not following."

"*Todd*." I'm not sure I like the way she sounds exasperated when she said my name that time. I watch as she begins tapping on her phone, a huge smile taking over her face. My favorite kind of smile on Donna. "You've been nominated for a NANA! Well, Hawk

Weaver has."

"Oh. Cool." I click my phone off and shove it in my pocket. "So where are we going to eat?"

"Oh, cool?" If I didn't know better, I would think she is mocking me. "Todd this is huge news. Do you know how hard it is to get acknowledged by NAN?"

"No. No I do not. I also don't know how long it will take for my taco to get in my belly, so let's go."

She rolls her eyes and slowly makes her way to the door, keeping her eyes on me over her shoulder. "You may be the first debut narrator to ever be nominated. You think people are clamoring to work with Hawk Weaver now. Just wait."

I groan loudly. "Aw man. I know I'm the best thing since Morgan Freeman voiced Go the Fuck to Sleep, but I don't have time to sort through a million more emails from desperate authors. You know they have a way with their words. It almost makes me feel bad for saying no."

Shutting the door after we walk through it, Donna makes quick work of locking it behind us. "First of all, remind me to look up that Morgan Freeman narration when we get back. It sounds amazing."

"You have no idea. It's my favorite book ever."

"Second, this is a really big deal, Todd. They have a huge awards ceremony for it every year. Red carpet. Stage and a podium. Thc whole nine yards."

I groan again.

"It's fun," she continues. "I love getting all dolled

up for it. Plus, if you win you can increase your rates with the publishers each time you consider a new contract."

"In that case, count me in," I say, making her laugh. What she doesn't know is why I'm so quick to have a change of heart. Money means nothing. "Wait, you said you can't wait to get all dolled up. Are you attending this year?"

Another huge smile spreads across her beautiful face before she says, "Sure am. My book was nominated too." She shimmies a little as she continues walking.

Looks like I'm going to the rama lama ding dong awards or whatever they're called. I'm not gonna miss a chance to see Donna in a strappy dress and sky-high heels.

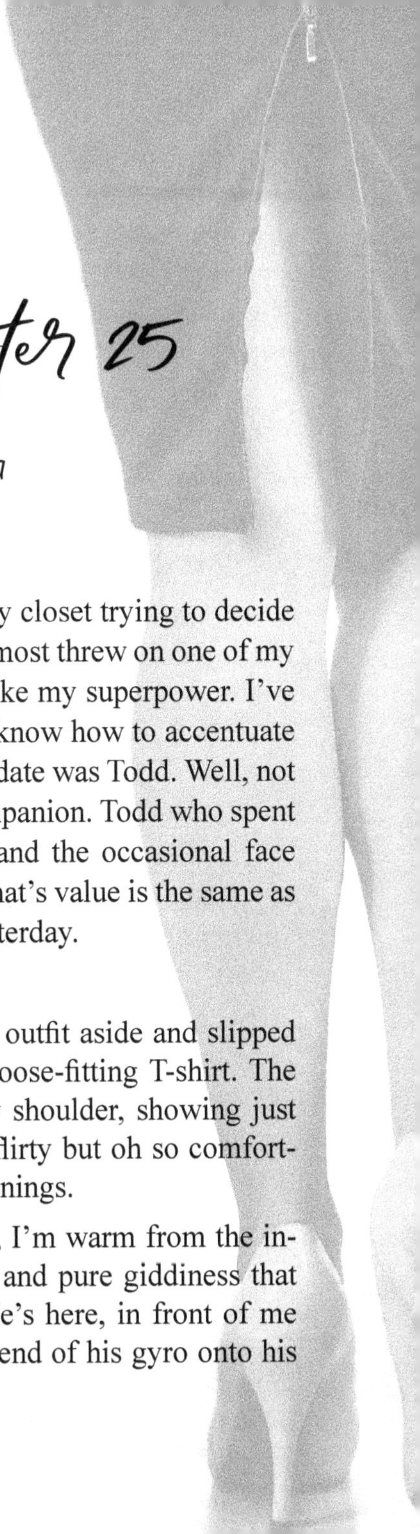

Chapter 25

Donna

When I stood in front of my closet trying to decide what to wear earlier, I almost threw on one of my date outfits. A pencil skirt is like my superpower. I've been blessed with curves and know how to accentuate them. Then I remembered my date was Todd. Well, not date necessarily but lunch companion. Todd who spent days with me in yoga pants and the occasional face mask. Todd who drives a car that's value is the same as the pair of shoes I ordered yesterday.

Todd.

I tossed the idea of a date outfit aside and slipped on my favorite shorts and a loose-fitting T-shirt. The neck is wide and falls off my shoulder, showing just the strap of my lacy bra. It's flirty but oh so comfortable for the warm Arizona evenings.

As I look across the table, I'm warm from the inside out. Nerves, excitement, and pure giddiness that he's here runs through me. He's here, in front of me with sauce dripping from the end of his gyro onto his hand as he uses it as a makeshift plate. I know he didn't come to Phoenix for me, but the fact that we're here together makes me happier than I've been in the weeks since I left our snowy bubble. My fingers itch to reach out and wipe the drops of sauce from his chin but I don't. That'd be weird. Right? Maybe? For sure.

"Here," I say, thrusting a pile of napkins his way. He mumbles what I assume is a "thank you" before wiping his face. Sipping from the straw of my iced tea, I smile as he lets out a deep groan of appreciation.

"You were right, Donna. This place is amazing."

"I know. I am in here at least twice a week for lunch. I can't get enough of it. And I only indulge in the baklava once a month." Of course, I buy an entire batch and nibble off it for the month, but I don't tell him that. "I can't believe you found a coupon online for this place. I didn't know they had them."

"Oh dear Donna. You must always search for online coupons. Those pennies add up quickly and soon you have enough for a free piece of that baklava."

He has a point. I wonder if I started tracking my savings and putting that difference away if I could save enough for that epic cat castle I was eyeing for Mr. Tuddles. I need to heed Todd's advice and start looking for a way to cut expenses. Not in my shoes or moisturizer but in things like eating out, I could easily start saving money. As a full-time author, it only takes one bad "glitch" or delay with a book release and I'm scrambling to make up the sales.

"What now?" Todd asks, pulling me from my thoughts. Looking up to him, I'm hit straight in the stomach with his smile. His dark hair is unkempt, and I want to brush it from his face. The dark eyes that dance with mischief on a regular basis look like melted chocolate and I can easily see losing myself in them for a very long time.

Who am I? Yes, I write romance, but I've never looked across the table of a fast food gyro restaurant at a man and wanted to wrap my body around his, kiss his full lips until my own are numb, and lock him in my bedroom for days.

"I, uh, want to walk a bit?" My voice is shaky, and I pray he didn't notice. Too late, the furrowed brows tells me he heard it.

"Let's roll." He stands and holds his hand out for me and as I place my palm atop his, I release a breath and gather my wits. Why am I so nervous?

"This place just gets better and better," Todd says as I slide out of the booth. Quirking a brow at him, he points to the ceiling. "JT." I pause and smile. It isn't the song that was playing the day I walked into the cabin and tried to kill him with my own version of self-defense but seems appropriate for where my thoughts are right now.

"I think JT was right. He did bring sexy back." My tone is flirty, and my heart is racing. Instead of releasing my hold on his hand, I lace our fingers and tug Todd out of the door of the restaurant.

We walk in silence, my hand in his, and enjoy the warm evening air. Like it was with Todd at the cabin, our quiet is comfortable. Compatible. We're compatible. Which is strange. He's nothing I knew I wanted and everything that I've needed. It's too much and too fast. It's ridiculous and completely out of character for me but I want him. I want him in my life as my friend and my . . . well, using that dreaded word—lover. Even thinking that word makes me shiver.

"Are you cold?" he asks, my shiver obvious to him.

"No, I'm good. Are you melting? I'm comfortable, but I'm in shorts." My words are rapid in an effort to distract him from the shiver observation.

Shrugging, he doesn't respond, which means he is probably burning up. I pick up the pace a little as we approach my building.

"Let's get you upstairs and into the air conditioning. I think I have a few cold beers in the fridge too."

"Now you're talking."

Todd opens the door to my building and releases my hand, ushering me ahead into the building. The cool air of the lobby sends goosebumps across my skin, and I wrap my arms around my stomach. This shiver is for the cool air and not the distasteful word I thought just a few minutes ago.

Pushing the button to call the elevator, I stiffen as Todd's body heat fills my bubble of personal space. His hands grip my upper arms and begin rubbing up and down. The friction sending a jolt of awareness to my lower belly. A quick intake of air and I stiffen as he whispers.

"So crazy the cool air can make you shiver when your skin is so warm."

And I'm a pile of goo. Melted chocolate right here

on the marble floors.

Before I can offer a retort, the elevator doors open and I step inside, pushing the seven button as Todd follows behind me. Standing side by side, we both look up at the number display. I doubt his mind is racing like mine. Thoughts of pushing him up against the wall of this elevator and throwing myself at him are the most vivid. By the time the display ticks to a five, I know I have to make a decision. We flirted, we kissed, and we cuddled in Idaho but here, tonight, I feel like we're at a turning point in our friendship. I want him. I want his lips on mine, his hands caressing my skin, and his body melting into my own.

I need his touch and his kindness.

Stepping off the elevator, I walk quickly to my front door and pull the key from my pocket. Slowly, I turn the key and open the door only to pause before stepping across the threshold. With a deep breath, I take a step and then another.

When the door closes, I don't allow myself more than a second to contemplate my next move. In two large steps, I throw my arms around his neck and my lips capture his. Startled at first, he doesn't kiss me back, and my heart falls. Regret is instant, and I wonder if I've made a mistake. But I don't sit with that feeling for long because his arms wrap around my waist, tugging my body flush to his. His mouth opens, and our kiss deepens. My heart soars and my panties dampen.

I'm a thirty-four-year-old woman and have kissed plenty of men in my life. Not a single kiss has sent my heart racing and my body into hyper drive like kissing

Todd Chimolski. Never have I wanted to crawl inside a man, to know not only what he's feeling but what he thinks. This man challenges me and puts me at ease all at the same time. His compassion and his humor force me to look at life through different lenses, and I want more. I need more.

His hands glide up my hips, one under my shirt and the other at the base of my neck. When his lips abandon mine, I let out a sound of frustration, but the moment they find my neck, with a slight flick of his tongue, my sound morph to one of passion and desire.

I release my grip from behind his neck and begin unbuttoning his shirt. When it opens another piece of thin cotton greets me. Groaning in frustration that I can't touch his skin, Todd laughs and steps back to discard not only his dress shirt but the damp undershirt stuck to his sweaty skin.

Eyes wide, I lick my lips in anticipation of touching his skin. Instead, of allowing me the opportunity, he grips the hem of my shirt and quickly pulls it over my head and tosses it behind me.

"Fuck," he grumbles as I smile. My breasts are full, and my nipples are hard in response to his gaze. Stepping up to me quickly, he tugs down a cup and sucks a nipple into his mouth. I'm pretty sure I've just died and gone to heaven. My fingers weave into his hair and I moan as he licks and nips. With a pop, he releases my nipple and lifts his head to face me.

"Donna." My name is a plead from his lips, and I place a chaste kiss to his lips.

"Make love to me, Todd."

Growling, he bends and lifts me by the waist, bringing my face even with his. Giggling, I fling my arms around his neck and hold on for dear life as he walks us to my bedroom. Setting me down inside the door, he turns to Mr. Tuddles who has followed us.

"Sorry, dude. This isn't a show."

The door closes, and I know what happens next will change everything. In all the best ways.

Two days of sex and laughter is by far the best workout I've ever experienced.

Two days with Todd in my world is by far the best life change I've ever experienced.

After the impromptu jumping I did, we've spent hours lying in bed talking and making love. And fucking. We've basically turned my body into a pretzel and while I'm paying the price right now, unable to get up from the couch, I've never felt better.

"I hate that you have to leave." I don't bother to hide my disappointment that his time in Phoenix is over.

"Don't guilt me. You know I'll stay."

"Would I be a horrible person to ask you to? I mean, you have an empire, why do you need more work?" Yes, I sound like a child, but I don't care. I like having him here. I like how he makes me feel. And I'm scared how I feel. My emotions and feelings for Todd are a rollercoaster, and while the high is the greatest feeling, the low is devastating and not one I'm used to.

"We need to talk about this," he replies.

Sighing, I fling my arm over my eyes and let out a deep sigh. Todd squeezes my feet that rest on his lap. When I don't shift, he pulls my hand from my eyes and smiles.

"There's nothing to talk about," I whisper before clearing my throat. "You live thousands of miles away. We're adults, and we can say we had a great time this weekend and that's that."

Liar.

"I think it's just bad timing. We're still friends though, right?"

"Of course, we're friends. You've easily become one of my best friends. I just . . . I'm being a girl. It'll pass." The smile I offer him is small and hopefully hides my disappointment.

Rising from the couch, Todd tugs my hands, pulling me to stand before him. Brushing the hair off my shoulders, he cups my face and places a series of small kisses on my lips. "It's just bad timing."

Nodding, I follow him to the door. As he's stepping into the hallway, I say, "I'll see you at the NANAs?"

"Yeah, for sure. Save me a dance?"

"Always."

Without another word or a kiss, he walks away, and I think he may have taken a piece of my heart with him.

Chapter 26

Todd

The NANAs are not at all what I expected. With an acronym like "NANA" I thought we'd show up to a community center somewhere and sit around circular tables that wobbled because one of the legs was a little too worn. Then someone standing at a podium would begin speaking, probably blow out our eardrums when the mic squealed. The nominees would be presented with a plaque for a job well done and we'd all enjoy a potluck. I was looking forward to some homemade deviled eggs.

That is not what the National Association of Narrators Awards are. First, and foremost, it's a black-tie event. When Aggi found out I was in the running for best debut narrator six weeks ago, she hounded me to get a tux. I thought I'd mosey on down to the local rental shop, but she went on one of her rants about investments and branding. I stopped listening at one point but did find myself standing on a box with a tailor becoming far too acquainted with my inseam. She still insists this is all because she doesn't want me to stand out in a bad way. I say it's because she likes torturing me. There is probably some truth to both theories.

Then, Spencer reserved a limo for us to ride in—me as the third wheel to their disgusting party of two—to the hotel that had the entrance blocked off just for this event. It was weird since we're actually staying at the same hotel the awards are being held at. We literally drove around the block in the name of "presentation."

But I suppose they weren't wrong. When we pulled up to the front of the hotel less than two minutes after getting in the back seat, we walked a red carpet that was well and truly red. Dozens of people stood in a long line taking pictures. These weren't the same women I met at the book signing. No, these were actual photographers taking pictures. With cameras. I have no idea who they are or what they're for. All I know is the cameras being used probably cost more than my last commission. When we settled ourselves around circular tables decorated with candles and glittery shit that sparkled when the flames moved, I knew this was much more than a potluck.

Since then, no microphone has squealed. No table has wobbled. This is definitely not my grandmother's award show. It's more like the Oscars without the A-listers and musical guests.

Although I thought I saw a B-list celebrity on the other side of the room. But still no deviled eggs. Talk about disappointing.

For whatever reason, the usher seated us at this table right in the middle of the room. If I happen to win, it's going to be really hard to walk through all the chairs to the stage. Not that people should complain about getting Todd-in-the-Box at eye level. But a man doesn't have anything without his dignity. And my deductive reasoning guesses the organizers already thought this through and the people who are actually going to win have a straight shot to the microphone. That's not me.

Eh. At least the flan is good. There's nothing more satisfying than caramel covered custard.

The only downside so far has been the company I'm keeping. I haven't had a reason to get up yet, except possibly to find a barf bag, thanks to Spencer and Aggi, pardon me . . . *Adeline Snow*, as I have been instructed to refer to her when she's at an event like this. Whatever she calls herself, I can't help but roll my eyes at how lovey-dovey my best friend and her betrothed are. It's even worse because they've been apart for the last couple of weeks due to her touring schedule and his physical therapy for his bum knee. Not that they keep their hands off each other normally.

In all fairness, they're not really that bad. I'd never admit it to Aggi, but I would be way more bored if I didn't get to poke fun at them every few minutes. Seriously. How many people do I know who have sat through an entire Oscar ceremony without losing their mind? None. That shit is long and boring, and they have comedians hosting. This shit has all the bore and none of the comedy, so I have my choice of entertainment: conversing with the lovebirds, or the old bat to my right.

Mrs. Buford is friendly enough in a stodgy, aristocratic, judgmental sort of way. She reminds me of Queen Elizabeth with her bouffant and powder blue pantsuit, except she doesn't smile as much. Her daughters-in-law aren't as hot either. I should know, I sat through thirty minutes of looking through pictures in a little accordion picture wallet thing. No lie, the second she opened it, it looked like a Slinky of pictures, each one more boring and pointless than the last.

She has yet to explain why she's here, and I can only assume it is for one of three reasons. She's either a publisher, an author, or a narrator. I don't want to think of this woman writing or saying the word "cock," so I've decided she's a publisher. Regardless, I should get an award for listening politely and not making smart remarks. That's just the kind of guy I am. Even if Aggi hadn't kicked me under the table I still would have been on my best behavior. You never know when these old ladies are going to turn on you and start beating you with an overstuffed purse. The last thing this face needs is "MK" shaped bruises. That would be hard to explain to my next client.

I'm pretty sure I should be paying attention because my category is up next, but I'm having a hard time focusing over Mrs. Buford's current tirade. She's been droning on for the last ten minutes about AM radio in her day, or something to that effect. I don't really know. I lost track around the time her husband interjected, and they began arguing over whether or not John Flynn and Virginia Moore, whoever they are, should have an honorary NANAs for their work on some 1950s radio show. It's the "origin of narration," they said.

For the record, this nana thinks John Flynn doesn't deserve an honorary NANA because he was a hooligan. Sounds like my kinda guy.

While they continue to argue, a presenter walks across the stage, black dress swishing behind her as she sways. I don't know who she is, but she has a bright smile on her face, obviously thrilled to be standing on the stage right now. She settles behind the podium, looks around the room as people quiet, including the Bufords, finally, and begins speaking.

"Good evening. My name is Rebecca Trepid. I'm pleased to be announcing the next award for best debut narrator."

Yep, it's my category all right. Aggi grabs my hand and squeezes in support. Or to keep me from doing something stupid. I'm not really sure.

"The nominees are: Hawk Weaver for his narration of *Extreme Adventures* by Adeline Snow . . ."

Polite applause ripples through the room and I do my best to look around and smile at people until one particular person catches my attention.

Donna.

Everything goes silent around me as I watch her clap and smile while the nominees are read. Her blonde waves cascade down her back, covering the skin that peeks out from under her slinky red dress. My entire brain stutters and shorts out by how beautiful she is. But that's not what holds my attention. No, I spoke to her briefly when we first arrived, so I know how amazing she looks.

What keeps me watching and from hearing anything else the presenter says is the way she's smiling at her date. Matthew, I think is his name.

What a normal, boring name. Probably for a normal, boring man even if he is a male model.

Matthew.

Even thinking about how it sounds makes me want to sneer. Never mind how he's touching Donna's arm right now.

But jokes on you, Matthew. Little do you know we text every day. And we talk sometimes. And she's been a wealth of information regarding Phoenix real estate, even if I could have gotten the information by asking some of my other connections. No, Matthew, I had real excuses to call her. We even video chatted when she got an advance CD copy of the narrated book. So you may be her date, Matthew. But I'm her friend.

Ohgod, I'm her friend. Have I been friend-zoned? There's no way. We had sex. Amazing, toe-curling, mind-blowing sex. Surely that means something, right? Just because she's talking to the guy and touching him and, and, *smiling* at him doesn't mean she has feelings for him, does it?

Good lord, I have got to stop hanging around with Spencer. Green might be a good color on me, but jealous bastard is not.

Besides, every Matthew I've known has been a giant asshat. This one is probably no exception. He'll probably try to get handsy later and Donna will kick him in the balls.

That sounds right. She'll go all karate chop on him and bring his ass to the floor, writhing in pain. Serves him right for having that stupid beautiful face with his stupid big smile and the stupid right amount of scruff on his face.

You won't be looking so handsome when you're grimacing in pain, will you Matthew?

Just the thought of it makes me chuckle. Not loud, but loud enough that I miss whatever is said before the room erupts into applause.

Looking around, I watch as some guy from Donna's table stands up and walks straight for the stairs by the stage.

"I'm so sorry," Aggi whispers in my ear. "You deserved it so much more than him."

I blink twice and turn to look at her. "What?"

Her eyebrows raise ever so slightly. "The award?" I continue my blank stare her direction until she rolls her eyes. "You lost."

"Oh."

Exasperated, Aggi shakes her head and turns her attention back to the stage. She seems genuinely puzzled that I didn't win, but had she noticed the placement of the tables, she would have seen the same pattern I did. Frankly, I'm disappointed in her inability to hypothesize just because her boyfriend is here.

It's obvious that tables in the middle of the room are for losers, as proven by the straight shot the man who currently holding a statue had. It's probably a good thing I didn't win, too. That dude has a lovely speech thanking his mother and everyone else in his life since first grade. I would have just taken the statue and made some joke like "Romance readers. Am I right?" It's better this way.

Poking at her arm to get her attention, Aggi bats my hand away in irritation. Mission accomplished. "What?" she hisses.

Pointing at her untouched dessert I ask, "Are you going to eat that?"

She rolls her eyes and pushes in my direction. This ceremony just got a hundred times better, now that I've had double dessert to drown my pitiful sensitive emotions in.

Fortunately, there are only a few more awards left before we're finally free from the never-ending speeches and clapping. Just in time too. My eyes were glazing over so hard I'm sure they would have been mistaken for donuts at any time.

Popping up from my chair as soon as music begins pipping through the speakers, I quickly try to make my escape. "Mr. and Mrs. Buford, it was lovely meeting you. Good luck getting that third son married off. I'm sure any blind dates you set him up with will be lovely." They nod back at me, murmuring their appreciation or whatever. "Spencer, Aggi, I'll see ya later."

Aggi places her hand on my arm, stopping me. "Where are you going?"

Standing up straight, I button my jacket and straighten my bow tie. "I have places to go and people to see." Gently placing a kiss on her cheek I add,

"Don't wait up," and wink at her as I walk away.

As predicted, my crotch ends up in the hands of a few more people than I planned, mostly by accident but I'm not convinced old Mr. Hannivan didn't cop a feel on purpose. Word on the street is he's a big perv and always looking for opportunity. Romance readers. Am I right?

Nope. Still doesn't work, and it's still a good thing I lost.

Eyes on my target, I make a B-line to Donna, who is laughing at something *Matthew* is saying to her. Seriously. Can he make it any more obvious what kind of man he is?

Clearing my throat as I approach, I catch Donna's attention. Her smile gets even bigger when she sees me.

Take that, Matthew.

Before she can speak, I reach my hand out in offering and bend slightly at the waist. "May I have this dance?" And nothing. Hoping I'm not bent over in front of nothing, I peer up to find Donna looking down at me.

Furrowing her brow a bit she says, "Um, I don't really know how to dance to this kind of music. Is it a waltz or . . .?"

Rising to my full height, I shrug. "Who knows. We can figure it out together."

Slowly, like she's reserving the right to change her mind at any minute, she places her small hand in mine and my entire body warms at her touch. Until she turns to talk to her date again.

"I'll be right back," she says kindly.

As she walks past me to the dance floor, I turn and give him my best glare. "No, she won't." Hurrying to catch up, I place my hand at the small of her exposed back and guide us to an open spot on the dance floor, which is basically the whole thing, since apparently no one knows how to dance to this beat either.

No matter. I don't care if the powers that be decide to play this classical stuff or crank up the heavy metal. I'm still going to hold Donna close and talk to her alone for the first time in weeks.

Plus, I'm really good at head banging, so that's not off the table just yet.

"I'm glad you decided to come." Donna holds her right hand in my left and wraps her other arm around my neck, my free hand resting on her lower back. Her exposed lower back. She absentmindedly begins playing with the short hairs near my collar and suddenly I'm grateful to be wearing this getup. It's hiding the goosebumps that have raised all over my body. "Are you having fun?"

"The flan was amazing."

She smiles and quirks one eyebrow up. "That's the only thing you've enjoyed about being here?"

"What can I say? I'm a simple guy. Custard makes me happy."

Donna laughs and between the sound and her fingers in my hair, I'm not sure I'm breathing normally anymore. It's this weird visceral reaction I have to her.

It's so much more intense than I have with my friends, and again, I'm praying I haven't been friend-zoned.

Suddenly her facial expression changes to one of disappointment. "I'm really sorry you didn't win."

"Don't be. My mother has been trying to get me to stop talking for years and they're trying to give me an award for it. They just undid years of parenting and don't even know it. To me, that's the gift that keeps on giving."

Donna smacks my arm lightly, laughing all the while. "You're a mess. I'm trying to be supportive and console you."

I shrug because I honestly can't understand why everyone is trying so hard to make me feel better when I don't feel bad at all. "It's not about winning for me, though. Sometimes I can just do something because I like it. If other people don't see the value in it, too bad. I did."

"That's a really mature way of thinking about it." She lets go of my hand and clasps both of hers behind my neck, pulling us closer and making me shift until my arms are wrapped around her waist. "I need to remember that before I read any of the reviews on my new sweet romance."

"Yeah, you should. Even if no one else thinks it's amazing, it doesn't take away from your value or your enjoyment of bringing the story to life. That's the most important part."

"See, that attitude right there is why you should have won. I must demand a recount." Her conviction is adorable.

"It won't make a difference. I hear the winner is one of the board member's nephews."

Her eyes widen at my remark. "Really?"

"No, but that's how rumors start. We could totally make it happen," I say with a conspiratorial grin.

She throws her head back and releases a laugh so hard, it echoes around the room. It's official, my new goal in life is to make that belly laugh happen again. And frequently.

"I'm going leave that one to you." She pulls away and I immediately miss the feeling of her body next to mine. "I'll be right back. I drank one too many glasses of wine during the ceremony and I've been waiting for it to be over for a while."

"Okay," I say as she walks away. "I'll be right here. Waiting."

She turns to look at me over her shoulder and winks at me, a playful smirk making her full lips quirk up just a bit.

Oh yeah. Matthew doesn't stand a chance.

Chapter 27

Donna

That man. I have no idea what it is about Todd, but he makes me giddy and nervous like a school girl. I've missed him over the last few weeks. Sure, we talk regularly and we've video chatted more than once. The days I didn't talk to him, the days he wasn't there to make me laugh or to remind me I am going to be okay taking a risk with this next release, those were hard on me. It amazes me how easily I've become dependent on him and his friendship.

Friendship. He's my best friend.

I wasn't lying when I said I had to use the restroom. Sure, I needed a break from being so close to him. The desire I feel for him has me all out of sorts. There's always been a certain connection, physical and otherwise, between us almost since the day in the airport lounge, but after our weekend in Phoenix everything changed. The connection we've shared became a power chord of lust. Feelings run through my veins and having my fingers in his hair, my chest against his with our hearts beating in tandem, it's almost too much.

That's why I excused myself. I need a breather. I need to splash some cold water on my wrists, take ten cleansing breaths, and toss a handful of mints in my mouth. A girl can never be too prepared.

Smiling and waving to colleagues as I walk through the room offers me a little extra time in my reprieve of one-on-one time with Todd, for that I'm grateful. As I round the corner to the hallway to the restroom, I see a familiar face and smile.

"Carrie!" I shout as I greet her with a huge hug. "What are you doing here?"

"Donna, ohmygod. This is so crazy and amazing. I won a contest on social media and am here with Pippa Worthington." Her squeal as she says Pippa's name almost shatters my eardrum, but her enthusiasm makes it all worthwhile. And who wouldn't be ecstatic? Pippa came out of obscurity as a fan-fiction author and hit the big time with her fantasy series about a girl who never knew she was part fae. The first cinematic installment came out a few months ago and is being eyed as the biggest blockbuster of the year.

"That's so great. Take advantage of it. This is a great opportunity to get some exposure for your blog."

Her eyes light up at the thought. "I know. As a reader I'm trying not to fangirl. But as a blogger, I really want to make a good impression, you know? I want to be included on her list of go-to reviewers."

"She'd be a fool not to see you that way. You're one of the most supportive people I know."

"That's so sweet of you to say. I just want to tell

people about books. That's it. I don't want to be part of any drama. The most heated debates I want to have are about which book boyfriend is the best."

"You do a really good job of staying positive. Even when some of us aren't quite on top of things. Like me. I know I owe you an email. I've been drowning in all this release promo stuff."

Carrie waves her hands dismissively and says, "I'm always willing to help, you know that. So," she whispers, "want to repay the favor?"

Confused I tilt my head waiting for her to continue. "Will you introduce me to Hawk Weaver? I know he's here with Adeline Snow and you're like besties or something. Please? Will you introduce me?"

Taken aback by her question, it takes me a minute to adjust my thinking from Todd to Hawk. "Oh, sure. Let me ask him first. He's pretty private when it comes to this kind of stuff." Really, I need to make sure he puts on a show for Carrie as Hawk Weaver.

"Yay! Okay, I'm probably going to get a glass of champagne at the bar. Also, I know this is kind of a weird request, but can you ask him to just talk to me with my back to him? I just want to hear his voice in person, I don't want a face. I feel like it will take away from the mystery."

Laughing, I nod my head in response. "So you didn't see him sitting at Adeline's table?"

She shakes her head. "From where I was sitting, I could only see the back of his head. Every time he would turn to talk to someone, I'd close my eyes."

Patting her arm, I can't help but laugh again. "I promise to come find you when I'm done, and I'll make sure he doesn't turn around."

Her eyes light up and she claps her hands. "Oh thank you. This night is getting better and better. Now I'm going to get liquored up. It makes his voice even better." All I can think as she walks away is that Todd will probably laugh hysterically when I tell him how excited she is to meet Hawk Weaver. And then he'll do some weird facial yoga before doing exactly what she asks and making her day.

Opening the door to the restroom, I quickly handle my business and wash my hands before standing in front of the mirror and confirming all my parts are sitting in this dress as they should be. I knew the moment I saw this dress online I had to own it. A deep red, the silky fabric lays just right on my ivory skin. The thin straps with gold accents crisscross down my back to meet the plunging back at my waist. It's risqué but still classy and on point with my brand. Minimal accessories and loose waves in my hair are the perfect complement to the dress.

As I'm checking the back of the dress to make sure the straps are in place, I overhear two girls talking over the stalls. While most of the attendees at this event are authors, narrators, and publishers, there are a few readers in attendance from giveaways and sweepstakes. By the gushing these two are doing about the hot male model in attendance, that would be Matthew, I assume they're readers.

When they exit their stalls still chatting, I step up

to the sink and wash my hands one more time before reaching for a paper towel, keeping my face turned away so they don't recognize me. Not that they necessarily would, but I have too much on my mind right now to be "on."

"I still can't believe we're here. It's so cool," the girl in a black sheath dress says to her friend.

"Totally cool. Sucks that my dreams have been shattered, though."

The response catches my attention, so I linger a little longer, drying my hands. Why would her dreams be shattered from attending this event? If I were a reader, or specifically, an audio listener I'd be freaking out.

"I still don't think he's too unfortunate looking. I mean, he's like as old as my dad but still not too bad."

Scoffing, black dress girl says, "He's not even close to your dad's age, but yeah. He ruined my fantasy. I imagined Hawk Weaver to be like tall and rugged. Long hair pulled into a man bun . . . NO!" Her shout startles me and I jump. "No. Not long hair. I thought he'd have perfectly styled hair, a five o'clock shadow that I'd absolutely pet like a puppy and piercing green eyes. Why doesn't he have green eyes? And his hair is not pet-able. Like at all. He's a total let down."

My rage is real. A pounding in my ears drowns out the rest of what they're saying. Words of disappointment over a man they don't know. A man who is kind and giving. He cares for more people than they'll ever know in their lives. How dare they not appreciate the man he is.

Taking a deep breath, I contemplate my next move. I should open the door and walk out. I should not say anything to these young girls. They don't realize who they're talking about. They aren't considering the fact that Todd, er Hawk, is a person—a real person. The same could be said for the authors in this room. We are more than they see online or that they read on our bios.

Clearing my throat, I wait for them to turn their attention to me. They don't. They're still chattering away about the dessert when I say, "Excuse me, ladies." Finally ceasing the debate on whether the dessert tonight was better than the one they normally get at their favorite Tex-Mex restaurant, they turn to face me.

"Ladies, I couldn't help but overhear you speaking of Hawk Weaver."

"Oh," black dress girl says. Yeah, *oh*.

"I just wanted to tell you that the man you are speaking of is wonderful. He is gracious, kind, and supportive of everyone in his life. He gives with his whole heart. When he laughs, it's like you can't help but join him. Quips and one-liners are his go-to response for everything, and it will make your darkest day light. And his smile. Girls, if you are ever lucky enough to have a man smile at you like he—" I stop and clear the lump forming in my throat. "Well, I hope you experience something as wonderful as his smile. So when you feel disappointed that maybe his look isn't exactly what you thought, or his weird pineapple shirt isn't what you ever thought your date would wear to lunch, remember how he makes you feel. How his smile makes you feel."

"Kelly, it's happening."

"Maggie, it is so happening."

I have no idea what it is happening, but I'm happy to have a name to replace "black dress girl." And, how fitting that her name is Kelly and she totally looks like Jennie Garth. Random.

"What is happening?" I ask both them and myself. Wiping my suddenly damp cheeks I wait for them to answer.

"It's that moment like in a book when the heroine realizes she's fallen in love."

Scrunching my face in confusion, I tilt my head as I try to process her words.

Smiling wide, Maggie, formerly known as "not black dress girl," says, "And it's when she goes to the hero, and he knows he's already fallen." Turning to Kelly she adds, "I knew these books weren't just fiction. This is why I'm holding out."

I don't fully process the last part of their conversation. I'm too busy realizing that if their assessment of this situation is true then I'm the heroine and Todd is the hero.

Todd is the hero.

I love Todd.

"Ohmygod, I love Todd!" I shout and turn to run from the restroom as I hear the girls says in unison, "Who is Todd?"

Rushing out the restroom, I run smack into a brick wall of man. Looking up, I see a smiling Matthew staring down at me.

"Girl, you left me all alone. Where have you been?"

Shit. Matthew is my date. I brought a date.

"I'm so sorry. I was dancing and then the not Jennie Garth girl was talking about heroes, and I realized it's Todd." It's like diarrhea of the mouth. I can't stop the words from spilling and realize I'm making next to no sense when Matthew starts laughing.

"Were you taking shots in the restroom? Are you on something?"

"What? No. I'm not on anything." Torn, I know I need to find Todd, but I also brought Matthew here and the least I can do is spend a little more time with him. "I'm sorry. I just really need to find someone."

"The guy you were dancing with?" Nodding, I look around his body toward the ballroom. Did they let in people off the street? Where did all these people come from?

"I think he left?"

"What?" I shout. "He left? No no no, he couldn't have left."

Shrugging, Matthew motions for me to follow him back to the ballroom. The party is in full effect, people are dancing, and I hear a lot of laugher wafting around us. Peering over people as best I can, I don't see Todd or Aggi anywhere. Spotting Carrie, I grab Matthew's hand and hightail it across the room to where she stands.

"Carrie!"

She turns to face me, a huge smile on her face. A smile that quickly fades when she sees Matthew. That is the strangest reaction to a male model I've ever seen. Not having time to assess her reaction, I say, "Have you seen To—I mean, Hawk?"

"Donna, how would I see Hawk? I don't know what he looks like." Oh, that's right.

"Right. Okay, have you seen Adeline? Spencer? I need to speak to them."

"Oh yeah, I saw them leave about five minutes ago. I heard them say something about warm sushi for lunch and then their friend rushed them out of here. They looked kind of green. I hope it's not food poisoning."

Dammit to hell, he left.

This really is like one of my books. Just when the heroine figures out she's in love with the hero, he blows out of town. Or in this case, an awards ceremony.

Chapter 28

Todd

I don't know when Aggi will learn that part of my charm is the ability to spot rancid seafood from a mile away. Maybe it's because I catch the beginnings of a popular cooking show at the tail end of The Voice sometimes. Maybe it's because I dated a girl who was in culinary school at one point. Maybe it's from my own bad experience with a fusion sushi roll. However it happened, when the words "I'm pretty sure that's not fresh salmon" come out of my mouth, the best course of action is to put down the chopsticks.

Did Aggi and Spencer do that? No. No they did not.

"You have to go. You *have* to, Spencer," Aggi mumbles behind her hand that is currently holding her mouth.

She's turning greener by the minute and I'm pretty sure she's about to blow. Literally. Turning my attention to my best friend, I point the bathroom of her suite. "Go, Agnes. Strip that dress and do not blow a chunk out here." Her eyes widen, and she runs toward the bathroom. She attempts to slam the door shut but instead, it only closes half-way.

"Get him out, Todd!"

Pivoting, I look at Spencer and assess him. He's looking gray but not nearly as sickly as Aggi. "Dude, you have to go. Here, take my card. Go to my room, fourteen eighty-one, let the woman pray to the porcelain gods in peace."

"Babe, why does Todd get to stay and help you? Let me help you, I really feel okay. Well except all the talk of puke. That's kind of doing a number on me." He grabs his stomach and lets out a rancid belch. I never thought I'd be able to say I was the sexiest one in the room when Spencer was around, but today appears to be that day.

"Todd gets to stay because he does not want to give me orgasms and spend quality time in my business. You know, my girl business. Now . . . oh no!" A loud squeal comes from the bathroom followed by, "Oh no."

I know that squeal and quickly usher Spencer from the room. The expression on his face tells me exactly how much he loves my best friend. Leaving her is killing him, but I've seen Aggi after too much tequila on spring break. This is not going to end well. No words are exchanged as I push him out the door. While she's in the bathroom saying "no" repeatedly, I pick up the phone and dial room service. I request a plate of crackers, fizzy soda, and a banana.

"Todd, come rub my back, please? That always makes me feel better."

"Girl, if you wanted that kind of best friend, you should've hooked up with Brandy Jackson. I'm not stepping foot in there. I love you more than anything, but right now think of me like that meme of the person consoling you with a broom." Groaning, she returns to her regularly scheduled program while I open and close suitcases until I find hers.

Rummaging through Aggi's bag, I pull out a tank top and sleep pants. When the toilet flushes, I toss in the clothes and say, "Brush your teeth and get your sick ass into those clothes."

"You can come in," she says.

"No way. I don't need to see your Underroos or, God forbid, your lady business. Plus, there's a possibility it's not food poisoning. I have important business to handle and cannot catch whatever you have."

The door opens, and she appears with a pathetic look on her face and mascara smeared down her cheeks. If there wasn't a chance I'd catch some exotic virus, I'd hug her. "To the bed, young lady. Here's the remote, I'm sure there's a horribly sappy movie for you to watch on television. Room service will—" I'm cut off by a knock on the door. Excellent. Quickly, I open the door and see not only the room service but a sad looking Spencer. Good grief this guy has it bad.

"Well, looks like your room service and your lady business service is here. I'm outta here. You two don't fight over the toilet." Without another word and like a man on a mission, I skirt around the porter and head for the elevators. I have bigger fish to fry right now—pun intended—than making sure they share the banana and the toilet. I have a date to sabotage and a woman to woo.

Stepping off the elevator into the crowd, I look around for the blonde waves and red dress. Donna shouldn't be too hard to find, considering she's the most beautiful woman here. Or at least she was. Damn. Where did all these people come from? Was the lobby always this full and I missed it? Or is another event about to begin?

Squeezing through people, I mumble my apologies and keep looking around. I better find her before the fire marshall kicks us out. Or she leaves.

Oh man, I hope she didn't leave. With *Matthew.* Just the thought makes me sneer and want to kick a wall or something manly like that.

Turning in a circle, I make one last attempt to find her, before giving up. Suddenly, as if the stars align at the exact right moment, I hear a faint "Todd!" over the dull roar of the crowd. My eyes shift to the direction my name came from and I hear it again, louder this time. "Todd!"

Just as I make eye contact with Donna, she surprises the shit out of me and launches herself into my arms.

"Whoa there, Donna. Have you been hitting the sauce while I was gone? Or did you just miss me?" I joke, but really, I'm confused by the feeling of desperation that seems to be rolling off of her.

Arms wrapped tightly around me, she begins rambling. "Kelly Taylor, but not really Kelly Taylor, was saying these things in the restroom and I confronted her and then she and her friend made me realize it was like one of my novels where the heroine realizes her feelings for the hero and it took me so long to realize I'm the heroine even though it's not really a novel and I had to come find you to tell you."

Oooookay. That was the longest run on sentence ever and it did not clear things up for me at all.

"Who the hell is Kelly Taylor?"

She pulls backs and gives me an incredulous look. "Kelly Taylor?" I stare back at her blankly. "Brenda's best friend who slept with Dylan?" Still nothing. "Have you never seen the old school episodes of Beverly Hills, 90210?"

"Not really my jam there, Donna."

"Weird. I thought everyone knew Jennie Garth."

That's the moment the lightbulb goes off in my head. "Oh she was on Dancing with the Stars."

Donna closes her eyes and shakes her head, mumbling, "I knew I should have opened with that."

"Okay so Jenni Garth was in the bathroom, or maybe she wasn't. But I didn't understand the rest."

Taking a deep breath, I watch as Donna straightens her spine and looks up at me. Clearly, this is about to be something important. I hope it's not that she realized she's in love with *Matthew*. That would totally suck.

"As long as I can remember, I have looked to find a life partner that has ticked off certain boxes. Smart. Successful. Handsome."

So far, this sounds an awful lot like a "It's not you, it's me" speech. Not what I was hoping for.

Don't start chopping onions just yet, Todd, I think to myself. You have to be able to see clearly to punch Matthew in the face. You don't have very good aim to begin with and don't need your vision to be blurry.

"I was so hyper focused on what I thought my ideal match was, I missed some very important boxes on that list."

I'm so confused now. "Wait, are you saying you're a lesbian?"

Now she looks confused. "What? Why do you think that?"

"You said you've been looking for a life partner. I just assumed."

"No." She shakes her head, exasperated. "No, I'm not saying any of this right. For someone who makes a living out of putting sentences together, I'm messing all of this up. Let me try again."

She opens her mouth to speak, and of course, *Matthew* shows up just in time to interrupt.

"Hey!" he says, a stupid beautiful smile crossing his stupid beautiful face. "I was looking for you. Everything okay?"

"It's about to be," Donna responds, flashing a bright smile at him. Any chopped onions have completely disappeared behind the white-hot rage I'm suddenly feeling. I know Donna can have any man she wants. That's her right and her choice. But dammit, I really wanted it to be me. "Matthew, I want you to meet Todd. He's one of my very best friends."

And my worst fear comes true right before my eyes and in front of my rival. I've been friend-zoned. My heart plummets, but I do my best to save face and hold my hand out for Matthew to shake.

"Oh yeah. The guy you've been talking about all night," Matthew says, gripping strongly with his stupid beautiful hand. Wait, what? Suddenly I realize what he just said, and my interest is piqued again. "It's nice to meet you, man. Donna speaks so highly of you."

I look at her, feeling a bit off kilter with this new information. She just shrugs coyly. "You're easy to brag about."

"Yeah, Donna was saying you buy all those fun shirts from a lady in your town that's trying to get a business off the ground. Does she have a website or something? I'm a single dad, so I love supporting other single parents. And my daughter would totally dig some of those tops if she makes kid sizes."

Now I'm really confused. And a little irritated. I am not supposed to like Matthew and his love of supporting small businesses. He's supposed to be arrogant and stuck up so I can hate his beautiful guts.

"Uh, I don't think so," I finally manage to get out. "But I can give you her info to contact her. She's a little pricey though. Trying to make ends meet and all."

He shrugs like it's no big deal. "Hey, if I've been blessed with the means to do things like this"—he gestures around the room at the obvious extravagance of the event.—"I might as well use it to help others. You can't take it with you, right?"

No seriously. I'm supposed to be punching him in the junk now for trying to make a play for Donna. I had no intention of finding common ground. Have I been drinking? Did I eat contaminated food too, and I'm hallucinating?

Fortunately, our small talk is cut off when another person joins our group. Unfortunately, this means I still have no idea what Donna was getting at before we were interrupted, and I'm getting more curious as this goes on.

"There you are!" the woman exclaims and grabs Donna's arm. "Have you talked to Hawk Weaver yet? I'm so excited to meet him."

Ah. My moment has come. This is where I excel . . . talking. Clearing my throat so I can bring Hawk to the surface, I reach my hand out to the woman in question. "Well, hello there. I'm Hawk Weaver."

A look of horror crosses her face, and she immediately throws her hands up yelling, "My eyes! My eyes!" She looks exactly like that scene in Friends where Phoebe accidentally sees Monica and Chandler having sex and it burns her retinas.

I mean, I know I have a face for radio, but sheesh. You don't have to announce it in front of my arch-nemesis-turned-new-best-friend and woman I'm trying to woo.

"Ohmygod, Carrie, I'm so sorry." Donna begins apologizing profusely which is yet another blow to my ego. Good thing I have self-confidence to spare because this is turning into an utter shit show. "Here, turn around and look at Matthew while Hawk talks behind you."

Quirking an eyebrow at Donna in question, she appears to have a sudden realization about the current situation at hand.

"Ohmygod, no!" she blurts out. "This all sounds so bad. Carrie loves audiobooks, but she never wants to see what the narrator looks like. It ruins the fantasy of the character for her."

"And yet, she's at an awards show for narrators?"

The woman named Carrie raises her arm over her shoulder. "Um, yes, I'm sorry, uh . . . whatever your name is. I kept my eyes closed a lot tonight. I'm sure people thought I was weird, I just have very strong visual images in my mind of characters, and I like them that way. I won't even see movie adaptations of books because I'm afraid it'll ruin the perfection in my head."

Odd, but plausible nonetheless. And definitely a better explanation than having a face only my mother can love.

Glancing up at Matthew he shrugs. "Romance readers. Am I right?"

Dammit. He even nailed my line.

Clearing my throat again, I say the only thing that comes to mind. "It's nice to meet you, Carrie. I'm Hawk Weaver. Forget the man you just saw. He is of no importance. Like that guy behind the curtain in the *Wizard of Oz*, or whatever. Thank you for being a fan. And I hope to never see you again. Because that's what you want. I think."

Carrie's hands clasp and go to her heart when she lets out a deep sigh. Huh? I was not expecting such a visceral reaction, but at least I know I haven't lost my touch.

Looking down when Donna grabs my forearm, I realize she hasn't finished what she wanted to say to me.

"Todd," she begins quietly, "I need to say this before I lose my nerve because the butterflies are fluttering like crazy in my stomach and I might throw up."

"Did you eat sushi, by chance?" It's a legitimate concern. Ask the lovebirds upstairs.

"No. But just . . . listen." She closes her eyes, takes a deep breath, purses her lips . . .

And let's out a shrill whistle.

I'm stunned. It's the language of my people. And she said it perfectly.

Eyes wide, I am singularly focused on her, despite Carrie throwing her hands over her ears and Matthew digging his finger in one ear grumbling "What the fuck was that?"

No, I can't tear my eyes away from the beautiful, smart, witty, creative woman in front of me, who just bared her soul to me.

"You learned bird language?" I whisper, and she nods in response. I need clarification, though. "And you love me? Me? Todd Chimolski with my weird shirts and bird language. You love . . . *me*? That's what you said?"

Another nod. "You, Todd. With your huge heart and your nonchalant way of helping people without a second thought. With your humor and your stellar ability to pick out a good cheese . . ."

I nod my head in agreement. I do love a good gouda.

As if in slow motion, we move toward each other, like magnets being pulled together. And I don't care that I'm thinking like a romance novel because this moment is everything I've wanted since I stepped foot in that cabin and Donna tried to go all jujitsu on me.

"I love you because you tick off all my boxes," she continues. "But I'm *in* love with you because you add so many more boxes I didn't know I had."

"I love you too," I whisper.

She smiles and nods. "I know."

That does it. We throw our arms around each other and the make-out session begins right here in the lobby. My arms tighten around her waist as hers tighten around my neck, and we suck face like a couple of teenagers on the dance floor at prom—without a care in the world and despite the glares from the chaperones around them.

I'm so engrossed in the feel of her in my arms, knowing she loves me, knowing this is just the beginning of something beautiful, that I barely register Mathew saying, "I think this might be our cue to exit. Care to join me for a drink?" and Carrie answering with, "Normally I'd say no, but under the really weird circumstances, I could use a shot of whiskey. But just know if you hit on me, I'm punching you in the junk."

No, I ignore everything around me because I don't want to ever forget any part of this. It's quite possibly the best moment of my entire life and I refuse to be distracted by the sounds of people around us saying things like "Aww," and "That's so sweet."

Because . . . romance readers. Am I right?

Chapter 29

Donna

I've always had my best night's sleep in a hotel room. Maybe it's the blackout curtains or it could be the huge bed and cranking air conditioner that sends me into such deep slumber that I wake up feeling like a million bucks. This morning, as I slowly open my eyes and stretch my arms in front of me, I give all the credit to the man stirring beside me.

My body revolts a little as I point my toes and stretch my body. Sore in all the best ways, I smile as I flip over to look at Todd. His dark hair is sticking out in every direction, begging for me to tame it, while the scruff that appeared overnight has me thinking very dirty thoughts. When his eyes open and connect with mine, I don't bother trying to hide the smile that takes over my face.

"Mornin' beautiful." God, that voice. The early morning raspiness makes my smile turn to a smirk as very sinful thoughts run through my mind. "I see your writer brain running wild."

"I love you." I've said those three words to him at least one hundred times since I whistled them in the lobby. Todd smiles at me, one as wide as the grin I was showing just moments ago, in response. His hand slides across my waist and tugs me toward him. Planting a slow kiss on my lips, I melt into him. Thoughts of morning breath, bed head, and last night's makeup are the furthest from my mind. This man, the way he makes me feel, and how deeply in love I am with him consumes me in every possible way.

Pulling back, he pushes the rogue hair off my face and grins, "I love you too. God, it feels good to say that aloud."

"Aloud?" I ask.

"Yeah, I've been whistling it for like two weeks. Come to think of it, I may need to explain my feelings to Bill. And you, my love, need to explain how you learned the language of my ancestors."

"Todd, you must know by now, when I'm under a deadline procrastination is my middle name. I watched hours and hours of videos to master three very important statements."

Throwing his head back, he laughs before allowing me to continue. "One: tacos are life. Two: yes I would like another glass of wine. And, of course: I love you."

Without allowing him to respond, I slip from his embrace and stroll to the bathroom in all my naked glory. With a whistle that simply tells me he appreciates the view, Todd jumps from the bed and joins me as I start the shower. The rumbling of both our stomachs cues me in that it may not be as early in the morning as I thought.

"Are you ready to do this?" Todd asks as we approach the hostess stand of the hotel's restaurant. When we got out of the shower and toweled off a few hours ago, I checked the time on my phone and noted we had slept most of the morning away and were quickly approaching lunchtime. I also had two missed calls and three text messages from Aggi. Watching as Todd checked his phone, I knew he, too, had missed her calls.

Looking up at him, I smile. "It's our coming out, how could I not be ready?" He lifts our joined hands to his lips and presses a kiss to the back of my hand. Seriously, has he always been this perfect? I'm swooning all over the place.

We're less than five steps from the table when I hear Aggi say, "You owe me fifty bucks, honey." Spencer groans, and I look to Todd for clarification. Instead, he shrugs and pulls out a chair for me to sit. Once I'm sitting, he takes the spot next to me and raises a brow at Aggi.

"Agnes, explain."

"I bet Spencer fifty bucks last night that my plan worked. He doubted my mad skills and thus, owes me fifty buckaroos." She bounces in her seat, a happy dance if I've ever seen one. Her confidence and pride are short-lived when she brings her fingers to her lips and swallows. Spencer's hand goes to her back as he leans in and whispers in her ear.

"Are you still sick?" Todd asks as he pours water from the carafe on the table into my glass.

"I'm better but I probably shouldn't jump around like that. It's going to be a long flight back to L.A.," she grumbles as she lays her head on Spencer's shoulder. "Regardless, I knew you two were sneaking around behind my back. Never doubt the Idaho mountains, folks. They are magical."

I can't argue with her there, so I don't. Although I seriously question that her "plan" had anything to do with my new and perfect relationship considering Todd's name hasn't even come up since we dropped something off at his building weeks ago. Still, I'll let her have this. Simply because fifty bucks is solid pedicure money and because you can't put a price on winning a bet with the significant other.

We spend the next hour catching up and regaling her with the CliffsNotes version of our love story. A time or two she tears up, I actually cry, and Todd tries to play it off like it's no big deal. When Spencer asks us what we're doing next, my new boyfriend surprises me with his response.

"I thought I'd convince this beautiful lady to come spend a little time with me in the Pacific Northwest. Maybe find some new inspiration for a new love story." His eyes are on me as he speaks, his hand playing with the hair on my shoulder.

Taking in his words, my instinct is to say I can't. My life is in Phoenix. Then I realize I *can* go with Todd. I have the luxury of working anywhere with electricity and Wi-Fi. A million things that need to be done run through my mind, and when I open my mouth to speak, Todd stops playing with my hair and tugs me toward him, placing a kiss to my temple.

"Stop thinking so hard, babe. We'll head back to Phoenix, tie up a few loose ends if you need to, grab Mr. Tuddles, and head back to the cabin for a few weeks. Or months. Summers in Idaho are beautiful, you may never want to leave."

"You included Mr. Tuddles," I whisper.

"I did. He's my homie, I'm all about rollin' with the homies. Plus he's not a bad staring contest competitor, and it's always good to have a practice partner."

Snorting, I say, "I love you."

Instead of responding, Todd pecks my lips once then twice as we ignore Aggi's claps as she whispers, "She loves him. Babe, they're in love". Then I say, "Summer is fine, but we are back in Phoenix by the first snowfall. I'm not freezing my ass off all winter."

Startling me, Todd's arm shoots up in a weird fist pump as he shouts, "Yes! I've always wanted to be a snowbird."

I've spent years trying to find the type of man I thought would bring balance and stability to my life. A man who was successful and handsome with ambition and a strong work ethic. I wrongly assumed that the man I envisioned for myself wore an expensive suit, drove an expensive car, and worked in a high-rise.

When I least expected it, and when I stopped looking, the universe brought a man who was all of that and more. Todd Chimolski was nothing I knew I needed but everything I always wanted.

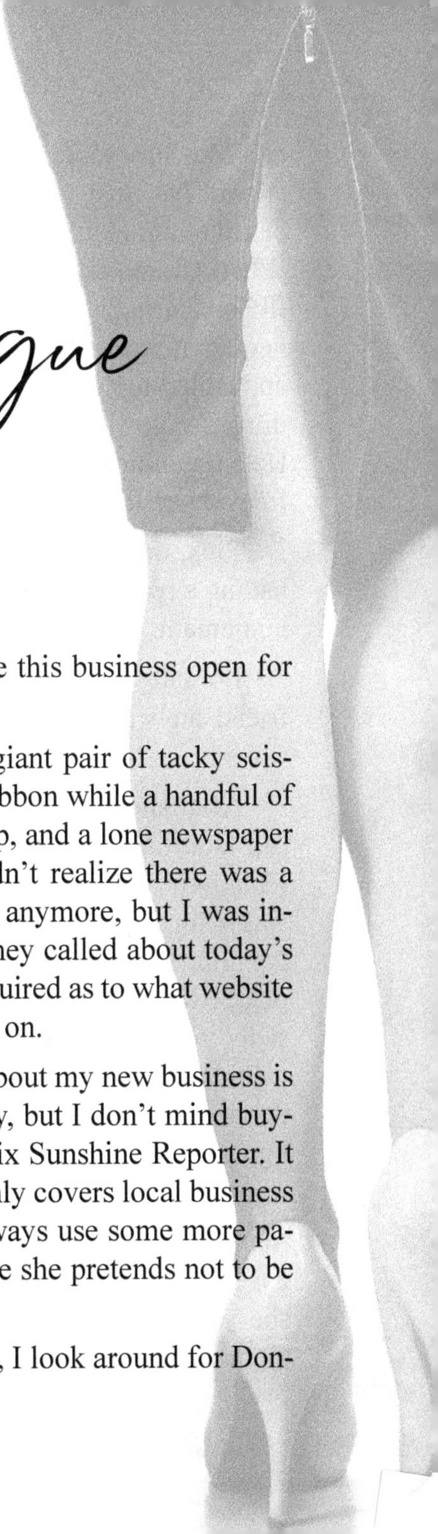

Epilogue

Todd

Nine months later . . .

"It is my pleasure to declare this business open for operation!"

The county clerk takes a giant pair of tacky scissors and cuts the giant tacky ribbon while a handful of local community members clap, and a lone newspaper reporter snaps a picture. I didn't realize there was a such thing as print newspaper anymore, but I was informed of my mistake when they called about today's event and I inappropriately inquired as to what website I could expect to see my name on.

I'm pretty sure an article about my new business is going to end up online anyway, but I don't mind buying a few copies of the Phoenix Sunshine Reporter. It may be a tiny operation that only covers local business events, but my mother can always use some more paper for the scrapbook about me she pretends not to be making.

As the clapping dies down, I look around for Donna, who has somehow disappeared in this very tiny crowd. Not that I expected a whole bunch of people or anything. Hell, I didn't even want to show up today. When Chimolski Realty started coming together, the ribbon cutting wasn't my idea. My silent business partner, Domingo, is not as silent as I originally anticipated and called the chamber of commerce to get the whole thing set up. It's been boring as hell and hotter than Hades standing on the sidewalk, but I'm always up for free advertising.

Plus, one of the community members insisted on having a reception after the ribbon cutting and brought homemade deviled eggs. Totally worth it.

Looking around, I still can't seem to find my girlfriend anywhere, but I'm sure she's around. She always is.

After she finally pulled her head out of her beautiful, taut, hard-as-a-rock ass, we spent the summer in Idaho—in the cabin, not the apartment building. Bill was a fine and worthy building mate for that time in my life. But I needed to move on with Donna, to a place where the insulation was better. Bill whistled sadly when I told him the news, but I assured him he would always be my building manager, no matter what the next flip project was. That made him whistle in delight.

Donna spent the summer prepping for her sweet romance book to be released. Being in my hometown gave her inspiration on different marketing ideas and she was even able to elicit Aggi's help. The two of them spent hours talking plot lines and characters. It got so monotonous I threatened to never narrate for either of them again. Did that make them change their ways? No. No it did not. Instead, they forced me to drive as they cruised around town, taking pictures for graphics. Well, Aggi took the pictures and Donna made the graphics. I think they both got a kick out of seeing a different side of their creativity.

As expected, some of Donna's fans were a little shell-shocked that she would ditch her tried-and-true hard-core erotic stories for something she called "fade to gray" whatever that means. She swears it has nothing to do with that book with a tie on the cover, but I'm still not sold. In true Donna fashion though, any time she was asked about the switch, she responded with "I'm not only one type of writer. There are a lot of layers to me. I just peeled some of them back so I could enjoy another kind of writing. Not everyone is going to like it. That's okay because I did."

Wonder who she got those wise words from? I should at least get a footnote or something.

Regardless, enough of her fans stuck with her and she picked up a new audience. So much so that she ended up hitting some sort of list for the first time. We celebrated the best way imaginable—in bed, naked, and with our mouths. At the same time. Fancy celebratory dinners are overrated anyway.

The next day, we went back to work. Donna started on a new story inspired by the mountains, and I continued finding solid agents to join my team and locating the perfect office space.

And as soon as the temps dropped into the twenties, we did exactly as promised and became snowbirds. Minus the RV and matching jogging suits.

We've been in Phoenix for five months now, getting my new business up and running and getting Donna back in "alpha billionaire mode." I keep asking if that means she's granting me some backdoor access soon. She simply laughs and tells me I'm *so* funny. Clearly sweet-romance Donna needs to take a hike for a while.

Now, as the sweat begins to slide down my crack, I realize we need to head back to my hometown and soon.

Giving up on looking for her, because clearly my eyesight is failing me, I bite my bottom lip, squeeze my lips together, and blow, letting out a shrill whistle asking where she's at.

Several people around me duck at the sound, which I don't understand. That didn't remotely sound like a car backfiring so what are they ducking from? Bird poop? A rogue pecking? People be crazy.

A quieter whistle calls back to me, and I ignore the odd stares and turn to walk through the open door where I find my girlfriend busy organizing the food platters. And she's standing in front of the deviled eggs, not allowing anyone else to see them except me. She knows me well.

"Sorry," she says, moving out of the way, allowing me to grab a delicious protein treat from the tray. "I was starting to get sweaty out there, so I decided to make myself useful inside instead."

"Tell me about it. I would highly recommend not licking my balls until I've showered tonight."

Her jaw drops, although I'm not sure why she's surprised by anything I say anymore, and she quickly looks around to see if anyone overheard me. This is yet another reason why it's good to speak bird. No one else knows what we're saying which more than makes up for people thinking we've lost our marbles.

"Todd! Don't say stuff like that in public."

"Why not?" I ask, grabbing another deviled egg. I need this recipe. These are amazing.

"You are surrounded by pillars of the community—"

"It's the county clerk, Donna."

"Only because the mayor couldn't come. You don't want to ruin your reputation before they have a chance to see what you and your team can do."

I eye her skeptically, taking another bite. Is that a bit of dill I taste? The zing is perfection. "It's your fault I'm already making bedroom plans," I accuse.

She crosses her arms, which pushes her boobs up—because *that's* gonna help my dirty thoughts—and scowls at me. "Oh I've got to hear this. Why is it my fault you're a perv?"

"Easy." I shrug. "You wore my favorite skirt and all I can think about is unzipping the back and peeling it off you."

She purses her lips, but I'm not fooled. She knows how much I love that outfit.

"Fine," she caves. "You win. But please try to only think dirty thoughts. No saying them out loud." I scowl at her. "Except in the bedroom," she clarifies.

"Can I whistle them?"

"Only if Bill can't hear you."

"Deal."

Coming closer, she wraps her arms around my neck and kisses the left-over creamy filling right off my lips before giving me a peck. Now I'm rock hard and have to think about Mr. Tuddles challenging me to a stare-off to get it under control. Seriously. I know she does this shit on purpose.

"I'm really proud of you, you know?"

Smiling down at her, I respond with, "I'm really proud of me too." Donna bursts out laughing, which makes me smile. There's nothing I love more than making her happy. "I know that sounds weird, but I think the new office turned out great. For a while I really wasn't sure it was going to come together, so yeah. Yeah, I'm kind of proud of myself."

She smiles brightly and pecks me quickly again. "So what's next? Another apartment building to flip? Another book to narrate? The world is your oyster, Todd Chimolski. What do you want to do?"

"No idea. Well, one idea."

She looks at me quizzically.

"We need to pack our shit and get back to Idaho before I melt into a tiny Todd-shaped puddle."

She laughs and nods. "Agreed. And I have another

story idea rolling around in my brain about a woman who meets her soul mate while staying in a cabin in the woods. I need some inspiration. Know any good narrators who might be interested in voicing the final product for me?"

"I think I know just the guy."

She pulls away and winks at me over her shoulder as someone walks in and my dream girl morphs into the perfect hostess. Man, I love that woman. I give her good ear candy, but she gives me good everything else.

Even Hawk Weaver would love how this romance turned out.

Ready for more Charitable Endeavors?

Add *Model Behavior* (Charitable Endeavors Book 3) to your TBR now!

http://bit.ly/ModelBehavior_GR

Acknowledgements

Erin Mallon – You are our favorite "ear candy" because you were so sweet to make yourself available to answer any question we had and give us guidance in the world of narration. Any mistakes are because we are forgetful and not because you didn't tell us. And since you're here, an extra special thank you from M.E. for providing a voice to her books, you are an absolute joy!

Karen L. – Thank you for buffing up Todd and Donna and making them shine. Oh and for making us feel like we're kind of funny.

Alyssa G. – How you were able to take "We have no real idea what we want" and turn it into this beautiful cover is beyond either of our comprehension. No really, we have no clue how you did it, but it's *perfection.* Thank you! OH! And can we talk about that logo? Home. Run.

Megan – You really are the very best thing to happen to both of us. We love you so much for all you do to keep us sane and organized. By organized, we mean telling us where to be and what to do. You are a gem.

Marisol – Why do you know so much? Seriously. You are the "phone a friend" contact if either of us ever make it on a game show. By the way --- get your ass to work.

Kristina B. – Thank you for joining our team and

helping us make this story even better.

M.E.'s mom – Or, should we call you "Eagle Eyes"? If that therapist gig doesn't work out, you should start a proofreading business. Todd just whistled he loves you.

Carter's Cheerleaders and Andrea's Sassy Romantics – There are no words to fully express our gratitude for your support of each of us and Charitable Endeavors. You are our biggest cheerleaders, even if you all are a little bit sassy. What's that? Oh yeah, Donna just whistled she loves you too!

About the Authors

M.E. Carter and Andrea Johnston are romance writers who share a love of the written word. Combining their sense of humor, beliefs in love, and sarcasm, this writing duo has joined forces to create the Charitable Endeavors series. With the sole purpose of bringing laughter and love to their readers while tapping into their charitable hearts, a portion of the release proceeds will be donated to charity.

Find Andrea Johnston on...

Website
www.andreajohnstonauthor.com

Facebook
www.facebook.com/AndreaJohnstonAuthor

Instagram
www.instagram.com/andrea_johnston15

Find M.E. Carter on...

Website
www.authormecarter.com

Facebook
www.facebook.com/authorMECarter

Instagram

www.instagram.com/authormecarter

Other books by Andrea Johnston

Country Road Series

Whiskey & Honey

Tequila & Tailgates

Martinis & Moonlight

Champagne & Forever

Bourbon & Bonfires

Standalones

Life Rewritten

The Break Series

I Don't: A Romantic Comedy

Small-Town Heart

Charitable Endeavors
(Collaborations with M.E. Carter)

Switch Stance

Ear Candy

Other books by M.E. Carter

Hart Series

Change of Hart

Hart to Heart

Matters of the Hart

Texas Mutiny Series

Juked

Groupie

Goalie

Megged

Deflected

#MyNewLife Series

Getting a Grip

Balance Check

Pride & Joie

Amazing Grayson

Charitable Endeavors
(Collaborations with Andrea Johnston)

Switch Stance

Ear Candy

CPSIA information can be obtained
at www.ICGtesting.com
Printed in the USA
FSHW021732080319
56100FS

9 781948 852166